The Tulsa Turnaround

ROB COOKE

This is a work of fiction. Names, places and events are based on the author's imagination. Any resemblance to actual events or people, living or dead, are strictly coincidental.

Thank you Kyra, Kevin, and Daniel.

Thank you Gloria Ogo and GO Edits Polished Editing for editing.

Dedicated to Paul Cotton, Rusty Young from Poco, who both passed away in 2021, and my mother.

Prologue:

Sara Barnum

Father died a gruesome death heading into Texas. My idol was a perfect father, who taught me more than I should have known about life. Hell, I hopped freights, chewed and smoked tobacco from a corn-cob pipe at age twelve. He taught me to play a guitar at an early age and, when we hopped the freight the first time, he showed me how to blow a harp. Mi Papi taught me more about life than anyone I knew. But he failed to talk to me about one thing: his heritage.

Certain details of my father's background were always hushed whenever my brother, Tomas Barnum, Miriam or me entered the room. It was like him and Grandpa Cecil hid some distant secret. My Mami was Mexican, Papi was Creole, I came from mixed origins and named after my father's gran grann Sara. I knew nothing about the woman except she was an interesting person who created the whiskey that Pawpaw Cecil and Daddy made.

My only regret before discovering later why he hated Texas so much. I snuck into Grandpa's parlor on a break from Grambling, where I attended college. With me was the Stella guitar that daddy found the day we picked up Miriam hitch hiking. I wrote Grandpa a song, though more interested in knowing about my namesake. Maybe I'd figure out something about our life, and why Daddy's was cut short.

"You wrote a new song over there in college and wanna play it for me?" Grandfather asked me.

"No, Pawpaw." Gran Grann Sara was on my mind. I realized I know nothing about her. "Can you tell me something about your manman?"

Grandfather's gaze checked the room. His lady friend was in the kitchen frying up some frog legs and making a pecan pie. "Sweetums, I don't want to tell no one any of this. I always wanted my kids to be good, honest people. There's a reason we can't cross the river over there. We got us a feud. Your Pa only knew part of the story and did not know what the truth was."

I peered at Grandpa Cecil. I always wondered about his father. "No one ever told me about your papa. You gotta story about him or how they met? I don't even know his name." I raised my arms and let them fall helplessly to my side.

Grandpa Cecil dropped another plug of tobacco in his corncob pipe, struck a match and watched it light. The pleasant pipe tobacco aroma enveloped the parlor room. Eyes closed; Grandpa rocked back in his favorite chair. He took a couple of puffs of tobacco, downed a shot of whiskey and smiled. "I don't drink much of this anymore, but every now and then I like a little snort." He nodded at my guitar. "You got that all tuned up in standard? Go strum along, while I tell you a story. You might want to write some of this down as well. Make a little song or a story. You're always good with words. Your Pa ain't never told you any of this, cause I never told him."

I twiddled the pegs of my guitar and strummed the E, A, and D pattern. Grandpa hit the pipe again, swallowed another glass of his shine, before turning his head to search for his woman. He wiggled his finger, encouraging me to scoot closer. The fragrant Perique tobacco in his pipe drew me closer to him.

"Keep strumming for a bit, sweetums, then grab a paper and pencil and write this down. Don't tell a soul, not even Tomas or Miriam."

Chapter 1

The War Between the States over the slaves set free, Kat Barnum returned to the States from Mexico, where her kind lived in freedom. A sneak across the border, plus a train ride from El Paso, now Kat searched for someone to aid in returning to her native Louisiana and her family.

Sara's father, Robert, had swiped the piece of property his uncle owned, galloped across Texas on horseback, with the aid of of two cousins, one a young Cletus Barnum, fleeing the country to Mexico and freedom. Young Sara, born in Mexico, never met her father. He fought for Mexico in The Battle of Puebla in 1862, and after receiving the news that some Yank blew his abolitionist father away right outside his small church, he returned home to fight for Louisiana in the battle of the states. They hung Robert for thievery and for being a traitor.

Born in Mexico in 1864, Sara migrated north with her mother after the surrender of the Confederacy. Frightened and starved, they traveled alone at night. A young Negress and her mulatto daughter would be fun pickings for any angry white male on their route. When they arrived at the states and crossed Texas, Kat, aware she and her daughter remained fugitives, sought assistance. It wasn't the aid of banditos, Texas Rangers, deputies, or ranchers. She knew someone of a higher authority. Certainly not the God her late father-in-law worshiped in his small Quaker Church west of Coushatta.

The disorganized underground railroad, plus the run-ins they had on their trek South, combined to ensure she couldn't trust any soul. Her family, West African descent and migrating north from the Caribbean, there was one soul she trusted for her protection. She hoped he would be in El Paso when she crossed the border.

Traveling with a small child all on her own, young Kat at twenty-six missed Robert desperately. She longed for his decisiveness, the speed of his horse. A smile crossed her cracked lips, since the kid could outride anyone. All she had to do was wrap her loving arms around him and clung to his chest as the steed galloped through the Texas night. They rode like holy hell across the border. Kat turned into a skillful rider out of necessity but riding like the wind wasn't an option. She traveled with a four-year-old girl. The best she could do was barter a couple of blankets and anything cash-worthy she could scrape up to get a train ticket home. The Frisco line would take her to Houston, then east through Beaumont and Lake Charles. She could steal a horse and ride home from there.

The ride through Texas was an all-day affair, but quicker than the way she last crossed the state. She sat at the depot, a stone's throw from the border and the river, her daughter by her side, both eying people scurrying off and on different trains, waiting for the one scheduled to take them North. With only a few pieces of fruit for her daughter and herself, she scraped up a few slabs of bread and some jerky for the oncoming trip. Once boarded, they sat close and waited for the departure, rationing their meals and nursing some water along the way.

The train chugged towards San Antonio and The Alamo, where thirty years earlier the Mexicans crushed the Republic of Texas. Kat Barnum sighed, enjoying her first free days as a Mexican. Little Sara Barnum, aged four, was a born in Mexico, a Mexican citizen as well.

Neither mother nor daughter cared about the history of the future landmark. Robert Barnum's widow and child wanted to get home. The girl slept on her mother's lap as the train roared north.

In San Antone, they intended to depart the short line and hop on one which would take them east across the mighty Sabine and back to Louisiana. Katherine Barnum imagined what freedom would mean. Would she be able to give her daughter an education, or will she have to struggle? Sara Barnum's Caucasian father and Negress mother had both fled Louisiana as fugitives. Sara was told this by her mother, but had never fully understood the consequences of her parents' action. Kat fell asleep against the window of the train, Sara on her lap as the night took over the South Texas sky.

Sleeping trains are no fun to rob. Bandits want to see the fear in the passengers' eyes. They want to see the elite shiver as they dropped their jewelry before walking down the aisle. The train stopped in Houston. between four and five a.m. and the passenger train sat waiting for daylight. After an hour's wait in Austin, named after the first president of The Republic of Texas, the next train rolled out of the depot. It took about 150 miles or three hours to roll up to their destination. Kat leaned forward, nose stuck against the window, looking over at the bayous and rice fields to the south side as the steel wheels whizzed by the trees and bays. Little Sara kept up pace, sleeping on her mother's lap as the train neared the town of Beaumont. The train screeched to a stop. The steel wheels created a sound like gunfire, the vibration sending Sara toppling from Kat's lap onto the train's floor and bouncing off the seat in front of her. She wobbled to her feet, regained her four-year-old composure and nestled next to her mother. Her eyes widened as Kat's arms clenched her tight.

Two men boarded from the rear, with another two blocking the front exit. One of the rear boarders was a tall kid, face hidden behind a bandana, and a slight glow emanating from his slanted eyes. He walked through the train cars collecting jewelry, coins and valuables, cocked pistol pointed at the whimpering passenger as he strolled up from behind.

"I need everything you have. All your possessions," the kid barked.

Kat held her daughter tighter, her stare fixed on the masked outlaw. Aside from her wide eyes, her face remained expressionless. Sara gave the man a similar look, the best mimic a toddler could give.

His gaze rested on the duo, and the slanted eyes softened for a second. The gunman pulled down the bandana off his face, revealing a small scar and a boyish feature that was a far cry from the crime he enacted. Though a white boy, he sported a darker, tanned complexion of one used to outdoor life. A soft grin appeared as his mouth widened, and yellow teeth jutted out. A gap winked from between his teeth.

"Never mind." He waved his gun non-threatening, pulled up the bandana and shoved it in the next passenger's face, robbing them blind and moving on up the car, stuffing everything into bags before hopping off the car.

"Mama?" Sara raised her head to catch her mother's eyes. She shook a bit.

"Yes, baby." Kat caressed her daughter under her chin. "Watcha need?"

"That man, why didn't he rob us?"

"He might have thought we had nothing."

"He smiled like he knew us from somewhere." Sara still peered up at her mother, her curiosity unwavering.

"Don't be silly. I have never seen that man before." Kat turned her head away to peer out into a rice field as the train started rolling again. It made Lake Charles in a little over an hour with no other incidents.

The mystical man with the straw hat sat waiting for Kat, who was oblivious to being watched, entered the Lake Charles market. Kat searched for some good fresh pipe tobacco. The man wasn't a choosy if desperate for a smoke, but when he had options, he wanted the best. Right now, he required the finest on the East side of the Sabine.

The woman entered the wooded trading post with no money and not much to trade with. She scrunched Sara's hand tight, a free woman in Louisiana, yet had never entered an establishment in this state with her freedoms, however small they may be. She glanced around the market.

"Can I help you, ma'am?" came the drawl from the man behind a counter. The man wore overalls and a white apron on top. He wiped the sweat off his brow, tipping his cap respectfully.

The store had seen many Negroes come in since the end of the war. Small-town merchants in this section of Louisiana didn't see black, Mexican, or white customers. They saw green, as the South was rebuilding from reconstruction. Kat glanced around, eyeballing the layout, in search of Perique, the finest tobacco from the Southern part of the state and rumored to be the best in the land. The Choctaw tribe cultivated and gave it to the slave families in a barter. While the white man raped for the privilege, the Acadians developed it, becoming one of the finest cash crops. The Yanks, bless their souls, harvested but did not destroy the crop, one of the few plants left unravished through the rape of the Confederacy.

"Have you got the Perique tobacco? My daddy wants some. We just got back from Texas." Sara still clung to her mother's hand, eyes wandering about. "I also need a bottle of whiskey. Just a small bottle. My daddy likes to drink it all at once."

The man grinned. "We all stocked up on it. You came to the right place. It's mighty expensive. You sure you got money for it?"

The smile turned into a frown. His soft eyes commenced their feverish glare. Even though she appeared to have no money, he bet she could trade something. He eyed the horse that waited outside. His second glance was towards the little girl. The final glance was up and down her torso. He smiled. The attractive Negress possessed something he desired. Not even being a husband, father, merchant and preacher could stop his sinful lusts of the emancipated slave woman.

Kat twisted her head towards the open door in time to spy the man she sought for help, the man who could aide her trip home. He looked so familiar she was sure she saw him in Brownsville, and again in Houston, but she never acknowledged him. He looked in and saw Kat's legs shaking. She knew what was going to happen to her. She was a kid on the plantation before Robert Barnum freed her, but already exposed to an older man's lusts, the overseer's infatuations, she was a victim at age thirteen. The merchant shared the look of the overseer. The similarity was so striking that Kat struggled not to scream.

"I picked me up some fresh okra from the previous town. I notice you don't have none lying around." The words were nothing she planned. Someone might have said them for her, even though her mouth formed the sentence.

The merchant glanced out the door. "Well, young lady, go bring the Okra in here, so we can work out a little trade. Maybe you got some fresh red beans as well. I'd be willing to give you three bags of my Perique and one of these bottles here." He turned around and showed her a medium-sized whiskey bottle. "For a pound of okra and two pounds of red beans." He wiped his brow, expectantly watching Kat clench Sara's hand and walk out towards the steed. The stranger was not in sight. She went to the saddlebag, but got no okra, and she had no red beans either. She had some pintos, enough to cook another meal or two for her and her child.

In the bag's pouch, astride the horse that would become theirs, sat some okra and red beans in a gunny sack. Kat returned to the market. She didn't wonder how it got there. She knew, though her daughter looked confused and hard-pressed to question her mother, but trusted her mother's instincts. Kat drug her inside. The deal was now complete, and the duo returned to the steed. The man was nowhere in sight, but had executed his duty. She stuffed the tobacco and whiskey in the saddlebag and, using the tricks her late husband taught her, rode out of town into the bayous of Southwest Louisiana. She had to be careful. Horror stories were still told.

He stood near an oak tree waiting for them as they rode into Leesville. A small plantation area surrounded by slave shacks. Sharecroppers attempted to make a living being free, remaining working like slaves to reconstruct the Yankee savaged land.

"I've been specting ya." He tipped his straw hat towards Kat, reserving a smile for the little girl. He caught the rein while they dismounted the faithful, speedy and sturdy horse.

Kat grabbed the goods out of the saddlebag, handed them to the mysterious man, who, without checking the content sat down to build a fire. Kat soaked the beans before cooking them up.

"You've been watching out for us, I see. Much appreciate it." She smiled at him.

"I appreciate this even more." He grabbed the tin of tobacco, took a small plug out, and stuffed it into his corncob pipe and then grabbed a match, struck it off some flint and took a deep draw on his pipe. He exhaled the smoke into a ring. She recognized the aroma as Robert's brand and missed the fragrance and her deceased husband even more. The man grabbed the bottle, devoured the container with his eyes. "This is mighty fine stuff. You got me everything I need. Where ya going to? I sure as hell can get you there, no problems."

The man knew her family, and he might have been the reason her escape years earlier was a success. She spoke silently to the spirits first. "You've been watching me; my family, and you will protect us from danger. Especially this little girl here. Keep her safe." She opened her eyes and looked over at the man. He acknowledged her silent message with a smile. "I want to get back to Coushatta and find my kin."

He raised his hat. "They're down by Colfax. After the war, they moved down there. Don't worry yourself none. I getcha der safe and sound to reunite with your kinfolk." He pulled the straw hat over his eyes, yawned without covering his mouth. His head resting against the tree, he went to sleep. Kat checked on the beans, and by this time, the legumes were ready. She stirred them up and checked on her little girl. Sara needed to eat, but she was curled up under a bedroll. She looked comfortable with a smile lurking on her face. Kat smiled and continued stirring the beans.

Chapter 2

Two days wandering through the bayous of Central Louisiana at night, the man, a drifter, a mysterious stranger but protector, guided Kat and Sara towards Colfax. Colfax, Louisiana, a predominantly Negro community, sat on the banks of the Red River, north of the bigger town of Alexandria. Because of many freed slaves moving into the community, coloreds gradually outnumbered the whites. The stranger felt this would be the ideal place for her family to reacquaint, where Kat and her little girl could begin a new life, a free life in the same country and state the former slave was born.

Colfax set up as a freedman town in a brand-new Parish, Grant Parish named after the General Grant. Founded by a Republican, Willie Calhoun, a plantation owner, who believed the freedmen had rights and gave the former slaves the right to vote, as well as a voice in state politics.

Neighboring Parishes, Winn and Rapides, remained mainly white, and skirmishes evolved. Before Kat and Sara arrived in Colfax, over thousand freedmen had been murdered in Grant Parish. Others, like Kat's father, Moses, fled. The elderly man approaching sixty left when the plantation he broke his back working on was burnt down by the Yanks.

With the cotton, chickens, and cattle all gone, Moses fled Louisiana after emancipation. No one knew where he went, but there was correspondence from him. It came from the Indian territory, now known as Oklahoma.

Kat's mother, Juliet, wasn't as lucky. With slavery, reconstruction, and being a well-endowed Negress, she caught cholera soon after Moses made his daring flee across Louisiana and Northeast Texas. Kat's family had departed. Brothers who fought for the Union lived up north, sisters raped and sold, and scattered throughout the South from Virginia, The Carolinas, and Georgia. Kat and Sara trotted through the forest until they came to a clearing on the edge. In the last tree line before the sleepy village, Sara shrieked after catching sight of a creature.

"Mama, did you see that?"

"Watcha talking about, baby girl?"

"I thought I saw a tree lady. The tree looked like she had eyes and thick curly hair." Sara did her best four-year-old description of a mythical creature. "She was banging on a tambourine."

Her mother tried to disregard her child's imagination, however deep inside she felt a presence as well. "I didn't see nothin," Kat brushed off her daughter's sighting.

"Mama, I saw this tree lady playing a tambourine. I did, I saw her." Young Sara pouted, clinging to her mother and trotting alongside her.

"I believe you, baby."

They followed the stranger into the village. Making their way across a clearing, the threesome rode into the village. Large wooden single-story houses greeted them. Families of at least a dozen people stood outside as if posing for the invention of a photograph. The people smiled at waved at the arriving strangers. Kat and Sara greeted them with a flip of their hand, not breaking pace, trotting on the mud road.

Soon the houses looked like huts and they came across a teenage girl, who must have received a vision they were arriving. She was bent over a wooden basin with a washboard washing clothes.

"Papa, welcome back. You got me some kinfolk with ya?" the young woman called out.

"I found them down in Lake Charles. Helped them all the way up here." The man refrained from telling her he was protecting the mother and daughter all the way from El Paso.

The stranger reintroduced Kat and Sara to the cousin, the remaining family in the area. "Dis here Mathilda. Not sure if you remember her or not. She always lived down here in Colfax."

Kat smiled, ran up, and wrapped her tired arms around the younger woman. Mathilda was wider, thick in the correct places, but hidden in a long dark dress that accented nothing. She wore a blue scarf on her pretty face. "You all grown, I see. Welcome to Colfax, Ms. Katherine. Sorry about your Robert." She went up to the lighter complected mulatto girl, pinched Sara's face, bent down and hugged the tired child. She squeezed the frail little child into her bosom. "This must be little Sara. She's gorgeous. Gonna break dem boy's hearts in time." She relinquished the grip but kept staring down at the girl. She looked at the drifter, the rescuer, and smiled back at her. The smile wasn't cordial, and it seemed like a plan was in motion. Mathilda walked over to the man, gave him a hug and a package. He disappeared towards the river surrounded by the large pecan trees, and soon the drifter vanished.

"You know that man, Mattie? He came up with me from Mexico." Kat looked back west towards the river. She eyed her cousin, wondering about her, and realizing she couldn't recall the girl from ten years earlier. Kat let Mathilda walk them, her first and second cousin, towards her shack.

The place was a wooden, small, three rooms with a mud floor. Three people inhabited inside this undersized dwelling, though they had a community supporting them. The Barnum family would live together with Anna Bourgeois, her first cousin.

Mattie was the concubine wife of Cletus Barnum, whose recent name change had him passing as Clarence Bourgeois. Cletus, a first cousin of Robert Barnum, aided in Kat's escape. While Robert, Kat, Cletus's older brother and Millie, the woman who he swiped, fled the country, Cletus hung out on the Sabine, aiding and fucking the female runaways. He took a liking to Mattie, married her, and she bore him three children. Two years earlier, he fled Louisiana and moved to Texas with their girls one evening. He returned one evening, told her his new name, and insisted that for them to be together, she would move to Texas and change her name. Mathilda refused to move, but she kept the name.

They settled into the shack that ten years earlier was home to slaves. Across the land, they set up a beautiful plantation home. Two stories, a large porch wrapping around it, and several bedrooms inside. Adjacent to the large home sat the foreseer's cabin, three times as big as where Kat, Mattie, and little Sara nestled. Their place was next to the outhouses, and a tad bigger.

Chapter 3

Colfax Massacre 1873

Racial tension escalated in 1872, at about the time the Republican William Pitt Kellogg won the election. The election over, the opposing party, the Democrats, sought revenge. A retribution that spurned the growth of white militia throughout Central Louisiana. Rivalries escalated between parties as Democrats recruited the militia to capture the Republican courthouse, taking back the county.

Springtime in Central Louisiana had the townsfolk preparing for Easter, alongside many of the Colfax men ducking downtown to aid in defense of the courthouse. A two-week standoff ensued, with neither side making a move, nor budging. Mathilda, Kat and Sara stayed huddled up, watching the men sneak towards the courthouse. They received gossip from the other women. Mostly skirmishes happened with nothing major for about a week. The white militia troops moved cannons in. On Easter, the leader of the militia accidentally was shot by one of his own men as reported.

Hell broke loose. One-hundred-and-fifty negroes died. Three whites lay wounded. Too hungry to remain indoors, Kat Barnum snuck out of their little hut in search of Easter dinner., In-between checking on the welfare of the community, she was out longer than expected.

"Mattie, Mattie!" Sara screamed at her second cousin. She grabbed her long dress and shook her. "Where's my mama? She should be back by now!" Tears cascaded down her face, adding moisture to the mud floors. Mathilda, in her early twenties, slapped the nine-year-old across the face, leaving a red imprint. Matilda shoved Sara across the room. She peeked out the window of the shanty. "I see people walking up the hill. They are tugging someone on a sled."

Mattie smiled, and it appeared sinister as Sara darted across the room to peer out the window.

"Mama!" Sara yelled, streaking out the door in the same breath, noting whose body was being drug up the hill. "Mama, no!" Shells continued stumbling as she reached the sled in which Kat's body was being drug.

"Run inside. They're still shooting at us." One man pulling Kat on the stretcher screamed at Sara. He picked up the crying girl, not minding as she beat his arms and kicked his thighs. Kat Barnum was dead, and no one knew who shot her. Whether the killing bullet had come from the whites or a friendly fire, Sara Barnum became an orphan. Over 160 blacks died, and three whites perished at the Colfax Riot.

Sara Barnum stayed near Colfax for another two years until she turned eleven. Mattie had vanished a few months after the slaughter. The times she wandered to the end of the village, Sara noticed the tree lady had disappeared and her young mind wondered if there was a connection. Since the community bonded together, growing stronger day by day, the village raised her. Strength and bonding were not what the whites and democrats wanted. More reinforcements were called in, incidents flared, and Sara had no protection, but left with the choice of either heading out in search of a new identity, or an old protector.

Midway riding out of Colfax, Sara heard the rhythms and jangles of the tambourine. The tree, she noticed, appeared to be in the shape of an African woman.

Beside the woman, chopping shrubbery, stood Mattie with a shiny machete that glistened silver. Sara pulled up the reins of the horse to halt the steed. Mattie said nothing, her eyes and machete slashing towards Sara. Sara glared at her cousin, who had abandoned her when she needed family. Their eyes locked and the stare down began, as if t at a game of poker. Mattie's machete flashed again, prompting Sara to instinctively reach into her pocket, only for her fingers to come away with no weapon. She bit a plug off her tobacco before replacing it in her pocket. The juice of the plant filling her mouth made her spit. The liquid aimed at her cousin fell short and nailed her boot. Sara kicked the horse in its kidneys and galloped off.

The kid wandered up alone on horseback along the Red River. Her deceased mother burnt by white men for being black. The trail cut through Pecan Trees that survived the catastrophe. Tall and gangly for an eleven-year-old, the orphan girl guided her pony through the unfamiliar territory. Taking her eyes off the mud path meandering through the trees and the river that flowed to the west of her, she glanced left to make sure it was still on her path. Clueless to where she headed, yet she never felt lost.

Colfax had seen the bloodiest uprising since the war that ripped the state and country, further dividing families, freeing slaves, but angering their white owners. Carpetbaggers, scalawags, and former confederates rode against one another, as did the freed slaves. Tall and scrawny, Sara Barnum fitted no description. Born to a former slave, a former thief and gray coat soldier. Her spotted pony trotted through a bayou, oblivious to any confrontation between the Democrats, who aimed to keep the freed people in their previous place, and the recent influx of the Republicans, all in favor of giving the former slaves human rights, rights women did not have, the right to vote.

The scalawags had momentum; the traditional former confederates had stubbornness. Much to the chagrin of most came the carpetbaggers from up north and the Yankees insisted on the best way of life for the people of Dixie. Sara Barnum belonged to no one and nowhere. They're existed communities for girls and boys like her, fathered by slave holder, born to a slave mother. She knew she was different. Alone by herself, there would be someone up the road. She sought peace within herself, peace in the land she would settle, and prayed to a God who listened to her silent plea. She recalled how she got here, through the aid of a strange dark-skinned man who moved in and out of the trees on horseback, never got messed with, and traveled without fear. Her mother had given up some whiskey and tobacco to the man. She wondered if he still protected her, or she needed to find the liquor and tobacco on her own.

She rode tall in the saddle, the horse trotting along the trail. Out from the behind a tree line, she saw a man, a straw hat covering his dark brown skin. A familiar stench of tobacco smoke filled the air, the leaf same that was made in the area for years. The girl rode cautiously. She jerked the reins, halting the pony. Both the horse and girl turned from side to side, and noticing the drifter, the horse retreated. Sara, straddling the steed, had no choice but to hang on. She trusted her pony's instinct. The horse spun ninety degrees, facing a small clearing that slashed through the bayou, away from the river. It fled, whining in fear in-between gallops.

In the bayous of west central Louisiana, anything could have startled the horse. The area seeped with wildlife that one doesn't want to run across, even though the wildlife is more afraid of intruders, and protects its territory once a stranger crosses it. Water moccasins and poisonous snakes snuck through the paths, prowling the grounds, and heading towards the wetlands.

This was the bayou, the swamps of Louisiana. There were no tambourine tapping trees here, and the bayous never slept in peace. Something always slithered through the night. Eleven-year-old Sara Barnum slithered across the swamps on the back of her sturdy pony. Her horse followed the narrow path, three-fourths narrower than the one they departed. The frightened animal showed its prowess, which is one reason her mother bought it in Lake Charles when it was a yearling. Nightfall crept up; the sun set behind the girl and her transportation, the sun flashing through the clearing between cypress and pecan trees. The horse paused, as if it gathered its thoughts. Sara looked around, following the steed's peering. She spotted a clearing in the distance. In its midst, humans performed a dance. Indians, she thought.

"I come in peace. I'm just a child. They must know I mean no harm," she murmured to the hesitant horse.

She tugged the reins back with ease, inching the horse forward towards the clearing. The Indians performed a dance ritual with drums pounding, and the small groups sang songs, which little Sara could not comprehend. The horse slackened its pace as the clearing got closer and the natives appearing larger as she made out their clothing.

Men danced in loin cloths that covered their lower private areas, women appeared in wrap-around dresses covering their chest down to their upper thighs. The rhythmic moves they created fascinated Sara. She tugged the reins, and the horse took in the events.

They crept forward, appearing harmless while celebrating on their land. Sara's people had their own night rituals. The banjo players plucked the gourds, while fiddle players danced around singing. This was like her life in Colfax. She gave her horse a soft kick as they rode up.

The chanting paused, and the rhythms adjusted to a more furious pace, in time with the riders' trots. The girl clung to the reins, while the natives shook their body to the speedy rhythms. Sara approached, and they turned to face her. They spoke in their native tongue. A language young Sara Barnum soon became familiar with.

"It is one of the lost elves. She came from the trees," One woman said.

"No. She would not be riding on that horse. She would slither in or walk to see what we are doing," a younger woman interjected.

Gossip penetrated the humid Central Louisiana atmosphere. Sara remained unspoken to and unacknowledged.

"Ku'aat," a girl younger than Sara finally said. Her smile, she welcomed Ms. Barnum into their land.

"Ku'aat?" Sara wondered if she said it right. Born in Mexico, it accustomed her to different languages and cultures, and already spoke English, Spanish, and knew some French living in her Creole home in Colfax. Sara hoped it was a cordial greeting as she leapt off her horse and strolled towards the girl. She watched the surroundings, paying attention to the movement of about twenty people focused on her.

An elder man, who appeared to be the leader, looked at her and smiled. Dressed in a loincloth, sporting a mohawk haircut, shaved on the sides, and a long black streak going past his shoulders. He spoke little English yet communicated with her.

"Ku'aat means hello." The soft smile on his face said it all. He figured she was a drifter. He knew about the issues with the white man down south. The girl must have fled and made a wrong turn in the thick bayou and became lost. The government forced his people to move. This band refused. It was possible they had a common enemy.

"Hell... hello." Sara looked up at the man. "I come in peace, and I am running. My mother, they killed her in that massacre. I need a place to stay. Do you understand?"

The smile remained. His eyes stayed on her. He turned, facing the small tribe of elders, young men, women, children, including the girl who told her hello earlier. He stepped away, paced himself towards the elders. The girl who said ku'aat followed him. He approached an elder, and they retreated into a small, dome-shaped grass hut they used as their home. Sara had no idea how many people shared the place. It looked roomier than the quarters she had back in Colfax.

Sara watched the men enter the hut. The little girl ran out. Stern words followed her exit. She waited, brushing her steed with her hand. The horse watched the goings on in the small refugee camp. The girl hoped they would allow her to stay. She yearned to learn the customs and was willing to grow. Her culture was already one of diversity. Born on the run, from an escaped slave and the thief who rescued her, she arrived in a foreign country surrounded by children and mothers who found themselves in similar situations. Sara's father was different. He was a Southern man, Louisianan, living in a horde of Negros and Mexican Indians. Sara learned to adapt at a ripe age. When she was eleven, she put her acquired knowledge to good use. Now she waited for the gentleman to return.

The voices inside the grassy hut escalated. She stroked her pony with more aggression. The horse jolted a bit but stayed put. Soon the man who spoke one of her languages returned in peace, as the Caddo were a docile tribe anyway. A small smile rested on his face, the mohawk haircut blew in the central Louisiana breeze. He walked toward the girl and her horse, past clay pottery removed from a fire and women cooking beans and corn. The smile increased as the distance shrunk between the man and the lass.

He whistled for the other girl, who greeted Sara with hello in her native tongue. She darted forward like an arrow. A hound chased after her as she weaved through the grounds. She caught up with the man who raised her since her father fled their Louisiana homeland before the war and headed to the Indian Nations, which would become the Oklahoma territory.

She stretched her hand towards Sara. "Ku'aat." Sara stretched her hand out and returned the greeting.

"Welcome to the Caddo," the man said. He put his arm on Sara's shoulder and led her to the group. Walking back to the small haven of Caddo, the man introduced himself. "My English name is John. I befriended the white man. They promised we would stay on our land. I think he called me John after a famous president or man in the bible. He said he had noble plans for me. He wanted to protect my people, that is why he moved them. I didn't want to go. This girl's name is Kaydence. I am teaching her English. She is learning fast."

Sara looked up at him. She trusted the man. Sincerity spilled out of him. "My name is Sara. Born in Mexico, I speak Spanish, a little French and English." She waited for an acknowledgment from the man and the girl. They stared at her. "My father," she glanced toward the ground, and back up at the man's soft eyes, "they killed him in the war. Blue coats got him. Daddy came up from Mexico to fight in the war. Blue bellies shot his father. His father, a man of the cloth, lived around here. They were poor, and he didn't believe people should own..."

The native interrupted her. "I think that was the man who befriended me. He was a kind person. I don't agree with him wanting to move us, but I think he wanted to, with a good heart. I told him I will try to adapt to the White Man's way and try to learn about your God and customs. I want peace."

This man knew her grandfather, a man she herself never met. She smiled and felt more at ease. "His son freed my mother from his brother's plantation. That's why I was born in Mexico, at least that is what my mother told me. I remember little about my father."

"I know your father. I believe his name was Robert. I worked with him, taught him to ride, and the White man said he rode like an Injun. That was a compliment to me. We often raced on horseback. The men were wrong. He didn't ride like an Injun. He rode better and faster. His horse and him were one, powered by the same God. Therefore, I accepted his father's invitation to study his Word."

Sara wondered if there was a reason she located there, if the spirits aiding their trip from Mexico placed her in this land of renegades. She let the man finish speaking, hoping he would acknowledge this.

The man tried hard to remember the name. It had been back in the 50s, before the war, that Robert and Kat made their dash. The talk was all over the land about slave stealing. He remembered Robert Barnum from the wanted posters plastered on Pecan Trees. The same trees Sara cut through on the way in. The trees that were not burnt by blue-bellies.

"Barnum?" he asked her.

Sara's eyes got big, browner than normal; her smile grew. There was some purpose in her being. She arrived here for a reason, as a legacy would form, beginning with her. Only eleven, and an orphan, her family legacy will be reborn through her. The man and women led her into the grass house. She walked in and sat down. New customs would be learned.

The Caddo created great arts with their pottery made from the soil. The Louisiana mud, perfect for the moldings. While the 1870s disappeared and the 1880s developed, Sara spent formative years with the Caddo, developing into a young woman. Sara matured as a Caddo, however, she remained Creole at heart. Sara soon grew up with the renegade tribe. They were at peace, as no one bothered them as long as they kept their place. They sent Sara into Natchitoches when the natives needed supplies. Maybe that was their intent, but Sara didn't have a clue. Marveled in the fact, the community accepted her as a young Creole woman. She fit in well with the band of refugees.

Chapter 4

Sara and Kaydence sat alone, each scratching their arms in the cone shaped grass hut. Sara swatted at her arms. She gleamed down at her friend, and her eyes twitched a bit. She swatted at the bugs again and nailed it as a splotch of blood appeared on her arm. Kaydence's eyes followed the splat her friend gave the insect.

"It's not the mosquitos making your skin itch," Kaydence said. "I heard the lost elves in the bayou. The same ones that brought you here. Your skin is itching, so you must leave us soon."

Sara sliced off a piece of tobacco, stuffed it in her pipe, lit the match, inhaled deep and blew the smoke out of her mouth. Her lips puckered as if she kissed the sky. "I'm restless, and my skin itches, so I can't stay here. I saw Coyote." She took another puff, inhaled deeper, held the smoke longer, and closed her eyes. "Caddi Ayo!" Her eyes shot open. "I. I…"

Kaydence finished her sentence. "You had another vision. It was coyote. I saw him too while you smoked. He's dangerous. I've seen him since you came. Maybe the white man is looking for you. You have to run."

"I can't put you and your people in danger any longer." Sara gathered her belongings. She packed all that could fit on horseback without slowing her steed down.

She headed out of the gap that entered to their hut. She stopped and shrieked. The two elders, and John, the English-speaking Caddo who welcomed her, stood there.

"Where are you headed?" he asked, his hands on her shoulders. "Caddi Ayo, their God sent a message to James." He nodded at the elder. The Elder returned the nod.

Sara did not give him time to continue. "I have to leave. I will cause your people harm if I stay and I'm not sure where I am going yet. It probably won't be far, and I will do what I can to protect you. I have to go underground, hide out in the trees, fight the carpet baggers, fight the southern White man, that won't stay in peace, the ones who want to keep the terrible war alive. That is why Coyote wanted me."

Kaydence snuck up behind her. "I'm coming with you. I know this land better than anyone. Better than my adopted father." She looked up at John. He glared back at her; he did not have to speak to tell her what he thought of the maiden's actions. His scowl replaced the casual smile.

Sara recognized the look as she spun back around and talked to her friend. "No, Coyote told me to go alone. I will be nearby. This is my place. This is your place as well. I will prove we can live peacefully amongst the white man, the scum carpetbaggers, and the men attempting to run you off this land. I will stay along the river, head South to the Coushatta. Bands of Coushatta reside scattered along the river. I have seen them in my visions. I will do what I can to help them too. This Coyote might guide me in the wrong direction, but he may be the spirit that led me here, but it is something I'm told to go alone."

A younger male went off to his grass hut. Sara watched him. I It was a boy who liked her, watched her, but was afraid to speak to her. He had observed the brown-haired girl from a distance, and Kaydence from a distance as well. He snuck into the tent and returned as quick as a deer, holding a long steel rod. As he approached, Sara realized it was a shotgun.

The girl had never shot a gun before, but there were many things she had failed to do before she arrived and settled amongst these good people.

Another young male came with her horse, a new speckled pony her hosts gave her. The boy put her roll on the back of her horse and tied it up tight. He shook it back and forth, making sure it was secure. By the time he finished, the other young man jogged towards the group. The gun in his hand pointed at the ground, and handed it to her and sprinted towards another hut, then returned with a package of shells. Joseph split the gun open, loaded up two shells in the double-barrel shotgun, and snapped it shut.

He looked at the girl they took in twelve years earlier. She had developed into a young woman, resembling a warrior princess sitting tall on horseback. Her hair blew in the Southern breeze, shells in the bag, knife in the sheath on her belt.

"This is for hunting, but if you have to hunt the white man, or whoever the enemy is, you must do it. Use your knife for smaller animals, and you know how to get alligator. We will scout your presence; we will alert you if safe for you to come home. This will always be home for you. This is your land as much as ours. Go, protect yourself, Ms. Sara, but first I need to talk to you in private."

She went into his hut.

He removed her hat, placed his hand on her head, and peered deep into her large brown eyes. "I understand you've been on your own and orphaned at a young age, but you are still a young woman." He swallowed. "There are men out there willing to take advantage of you."

She looked up and not smiling. "What do you mean?"

"You are a pretty young lady; many men out there are willing to capture you, trade you off, and sell you for purposes you would not like."

"I think I understand. This is one reason I'll be carrying both a knife and a shotgun."

"Yes," he replied. "However, killing a man should be an emergency only. You should kill to be spared being raped, killed or even sold off. Be confident when you talk. Look them straight in the eye. You must negotiate, always ask for more, never settle for something less than you deserve. If you are trading something worth fifty dollars, ask for seventy-five. Talk him up to the price you deserve."

She absorbed the information. "If he doesn't barter with me?"

"Walk away. There will be someone who will. More than likely, he will. He needs goods, like you do. A trader, a shopkeeper makes his living this way. If he loses a bit on you, he can take advantage of someone else. This is what they do, so believe me, I've had this done to me before. Remember, I'm giving you lessons I've learned myself."

"Is that all, sir?"

"No, Ms. Sara. You are a child to many, and a stranger doesn't know your experience. I'm glad I do, but don't be nervous when greeting. Look them straight in the eye. Talk facts. Get to the point and avoid small talk unless you're selling something. If you have to sell property, furs, meat you have killed, you want to embellish to get the best price. I know you will do fine. I understand you have to go. The spirits have told me so, but I comprehend you, and the spirits will protect our little group here. I'm not sure about the white man, either the blue or gray coats both want us off their land, like they want your people off your land you worked for."

"I'm protecting you. Your family and your people took me in when I was riding the trails. I heard The Little Elves speak to me to follow them, to hide me from Coyote and the White Man. They taught me to seek shelter here. Now the Coyote, or the White Man, has discovered me, and I can't put you in danger. I don't know why they seek me. It must be because of my father, the man they say was a thief."

She pulled up the reins, kicked her horse with her right heel. The steed turned and soon galloped off towards the river. Sara would hide in the bayous, riding along the Red River. She would seek justice and craved revenge.

Chapter 5

Sara spent her early twenties on the run as a fugitive, learning survival skills, rode at night, hid in the day. The bayous along the river, she could hide, fish, trap, and hunt. She trotted down the riverside between Natchitoches and Colfax, seeking the Democrats for killing her mother, the blue bellies for killing her people and savaging the land. She hated the carpet baggers for ripping up the heritage. Everyone was misunderstood during this reconstructive period. There were no good guys, except the peaceful people she left, and the former slaves, and the Caddo that took her in.

Rumor floating around was that a gang of misfits was out there killing travelers on a pilgrimage across the great state to places further west across the haunted rivers. Some pilgrims made their destination in Texas. Others never made it through the bayou, at least they never made it out alive. When she returned to Colfax, she sought to gather courage to seek her mother's grave. The tree-woman remained. Mattie was nowhere in sight.

She rode into the village of former slaves, scratching out a living, delivering ice, working their own land, or working the plantations, housekeeping, basically what they did before the war. This time they saved the pennies they earned, hoping to purchase their own land, acquire schools to read, write and educate.

"My lady, that lil Sara all grown up," an older colored woman said as Sara rode up on the steed, dressed in a deerskin vest, shells in her pocket, and flaunting a flat-topped cowboy hat. Her dark hair flowed well past her shoulders. She didn't smile. Her mission here was refueling, food gathering, and a mission of peace. She would soon return to a land which made her comfortable. The swamps of Louisiana.

"Mama McBee, yes, it's me. I'm all grown and checking on ya folks. I want to see where you laid my poor Mama." She got off the horse, the shotgun at her side. She paced around the shanties, peering around to see if she recognized anyone.

"You ain't grown or nothing. Chil' you ain't nothin' but a big kid right now. You ain't had no kids yet, had you?"

"No, ma'am. I ain't gonna have none either. I'm ready to take back this place." She cocked her shotgun, pointed it at nothing, aimed but didn't pull the trigger.

"Now you just showing foolishness. You still a kid if you ain't got none of your own. Playing with those things, don't make you grown, it makes you a fool. Now if you stay here, we need you to help us out with some farmin'." Mama McBee dug her hoe into the ground deeper, digging up more Louisiana mud. "We all work around here, so the youngins can go to school. That's the place you should be at. Teaches you to read and write." She turned her head back down, facing the dirt, and kept working.

"Ah hell, I can read and write, speak four languages. I need a place to practice this shotgun before I ride out again to protect my other folks. Sara glanced around. Older folks scattered about, little children ran amuck, forcing her relocation for immediate target practice.

She looked back at Mama McBee. The stout woman, overdressed in a long-flowered dress, wiped her brow with her headband. Sara didn't say goodbye, acknowledged no one else, but focused on something that could be target practice, a tin can, anything. She kept up her pace, picking things up and tossing them airborne.

She'd never shot a gun in her life; and needed a bigger target for her first shot. She found it. A large tin can nestled by a burned-out campfire. The logs sat in half ashes, not smoldering. Sara kicked the logs before reaching down to pick up the can from the pit. She watched it roll away from the villagers and strolled to pick the storage container up. Sara eyed it like a prize raccoon trapped for the Caddo and ventured into a clearing. She set the can down on a stump, retreated a safe distance, maybe twenty-five yards for her initial shot. She'd back up further for subsequent shots.

She nestled the butt of the gun against her shoulder, closed her left eye, the right eye concentrating on the large can. Her finger itched as it felt the front trigger. Her double barrel had two triggers. The kick of the gun knocked her flat on her backside as she pulled them both. Sara inspected the fallen can. She admired the holes in it. They were near the side of the can, not a bull's eye. Counting ten more strides, she placed the cannister on the ground and retreated to her original shooting point. She cracked the gun butt, placed two shells in, and snapped the gun together. She exhaled.

"This is a tin can I'm shooting up. Relax, Sara." Her arm steadied, her left eye closed, the other eye focused on the target. The blast forced her to retreat. The can went backwards. She walked up to the can, noticed the holes in the center and gave the shot up can a soft kiss.

"Sara Barnum, you're a natural. You found your calling."

Her horse remained tied up one hundred yards away. It watched her move the can again. She wanted another ten yards' distance. She aimed quicker from various angles. Her future endeavors would need quick shots from her knees, from the swamp and the ground were required. She practiced all, nailed a few squirrels, raccoons, possums, and rabbits for good measure.

She sat by the small campfire she made. Berries had been picked and rinsed in the river, the dead animal pelts hung out to dry, the meat cooked. Rabbit made an excellent dinner as she feasted, tossing the bones into the fire. The sinister smile on her face increased as she watched each bone burn. She thought of her mother, father, and the grandparents she never had the privilege of meeting. Two she knew were dead, the other two she was clueless about their identity. They might have been sold off, sent across country before she was born. They may have died before the massacre. She wished she knew, but there was one reason she didn't know. That was the pre-war institution.

Her bedroll unwrapped, she nestled below a pecan tree, and pulled her hat over her eyes. Bullfrogs moaned out sweet sounds of the swamp, a perfect rhythm like a music combo, and the songs they sang soothed her. She pulled her hat down over her head, closed her eyes, and dreamt of her upcoming life.

The following morning, she gathered more berries, skinned and cleaned a rabbit that had suckered into one of her traps. She had breakfast over the fire before practicing her craft once again. She shot from her knees, onto the ground, running and stopping behind trees, pointing and aiming. The tin never stood a chance as she made good on her shots. More practice was required after she visited the trading post.

She boarded her steed, bedroll attached, and galloped towards the market. It was a mile up the river, right by the ferry crossing. She noticed the stage coming. The team of six powerful horses pulled the large wagon towards the raft that would receive a tug across the Red River. Pulling back on the reins, she guided her companion behind a stretched-out tree line and pulled her binoculars to observe the pilgrims. She watched them board the ferry.

The oak of the man who pulled the ferry across the Red River was tall, strong, and dark-skinned, eking out a living by using his brute strength to aid the family out of the stagecoach so they could stretch their legs. She counted a man, a woman with three children. She assumed they were together, from somewhere back east and heading to Texas.

The family appeared harmless, however, her future profession required one hundred percent anonymity. No one, except for a trader at a river market, would see her face.

Sara, needing to over-trade with the person who ran the market, needed to have his trust. Unaware of how many pelts it would take for several boxes of shotgun shells, she didn't prepare the numbers, however; she was ready for worse. The last two shells remained in the shotgun. Same reason she hid from the pilgrims.

The kids ran into the store before their parents, desiring some sort of treat their family spoiled them with back east. The brats screamed their way into the trading post, colliding with a man as he exited. "No excuse me," said the man with a glare. "Damn kids, watch where you're going! I ought to take you to the river and whip your behinds. If you was my kids, that's what I'll do."

Sara watched with the field glasses as the kid's parents came up. Both dressed in fancy clothes, too fancy for West Central Louisiana. The large Caucasian man in a flat cowboy hat, similar to Sara's, was stocky, had a handlebar mustache. He dressed nicer than most of the men in town and turned his focus on the parents. "Them your kids?" He stood in the man's face.

"Yes, they are," the man told him. "Lovely children, don't you say?" He smiled, proud of his youngins.

The customer cut off a piece of tobacco, placed it in his mouth, chomped on it with passion and fury. He turned and spat at the aristocrat's feet. "Keep dem brats on a leash. They nearly ran me over." He walked to his horse and got on, riding into the forest towards the white part of Louisiana.

Sara crept closer to the store, hat down, covering her eyes, with little of her face exposed, and waited for the family to exit the premises. She glanced around, saw the man cut through the bayou. She raised her field glasses again, and spied him slashing through an opening in the forest, and then disappeared.

When he failed to reappear, she went back to watching for the family to exit. The kids came running out, sucking on striped candies. The mother walked out with a small bag, while the father pulled the rest of the goods onto a small wagon. He loaded them on the back of the stagecoach, then aided his children and his wife inside the coach. Sara shook her head at the woman. Climbing in that thing was easy, since only a high brow dame needed a helping hand. She watched the father climb aboard the coach and take the reins. Soon they rode off in the same direction as the man. Once they passed her, Sara rode up. She tied her horse to the hitching post and strolled in carrying the pelts, her shotgun with the two shells nestled inside and ready-to-use if necessary.

"Hey, young lady, new around here?" the man spoke to her. He was tall, gray beard, and a balding head and dressed in a plain white shirt with suspenders. Nothing said he was a dangerous man, only a businessman running a shop, trying to eek a living out in the Bayou during reconstruction. Sara glanced around, checking to see if there were other patrons shopping.

Lucky she was alone except for the shopkeeper. "I'm from nearby. Did some hunting and trapping. Got me some nice pelts, and I'm ready to make a deal. You do trade, don't ya?" Her hat still covered most of her face, but she looked up at him. Her attempt to be sincere.

He glanced over the pelts; a small smile came on his face. He was used to this game. Trappers came in all the time, trading for supplies. He noticed the girl's face, then spotted the gun. She was a stranger. He kept his guard up and sighed. "Watcha want for all those pelts?"

"I need me some shells, a bunch of them. Maybe a rifle and a slew of bullets. I'm going off West, maybe to Texas. I think I got family out there." What can I get for this? "I got some more meat you can cure up, make some jerky. Fresh, got them last night and this morning. Plus, I need a pipe, some tobacco, the good local kind, and a nice bottle of your best whiskey."

"A little young to be drinking this stuff, ain't ya?" The man grabbed a local brew, "brought in by some locals." He opened the bottle, poured her a shot, and shoved it across the counter. "Let me see if the little girl can take it, then I'll give you the entire bottle."

Sara, a non-drinker, had done some shots of whiskey. She drank a glass of wine on occasion before she rambled out of Colfax but hadn't touched it with the Caddo. For the most part, they weren't indulging. The government knew of their existence. As long as they kept their peace, they could stay on the land. But for any reason to eradicate their well-being, the government waited, ready to pounce like a cat on a mouse. Feds never needed an excuse to eradicate a native nation.

"This might not be for me, but I'll take that snort, anyway." She sniffed the shot glass, making a face. She closed her eyes, winced, and shook her head before pouring it down. It burned all the way. She took another gulp and slammed the glass down. "Okay, I'll take ya up on that. Now, I'll take that Perique tobacco, and that corncob pipe over there, plus four boxes of shells…" She eyed a rifle setting in back. It resembled a Winchester. "I'll get that rifle and a bunch of bullets. I gotta cross Texas. The family settled near El Paso. I hear that's a mighty long way across da state."

The man smiled. "Clear across that damn state. Pretty little girl needs to watch out. Indians ain't nothing like the peaceful ones scattered about here. Still think they should all be gone. But if they come in peace, I'll serve them. If they cause problems, I got this." He picked a revolver from behind the counter, pointing the weapon at her.

She stared him down until he relaxed. "I'll take five more pelts, and everything is yours."

She exited the store with her belongings short of her rifle. After packing up, she grabbed five more racoon pelts, reentered the establishment and pranced up to the man. She dropped the fur off. "I'll go get the gun myself and see myself out."

She grabbed the rifle, her hand on her hat, careful not to tip it to the man, but in a cordial gesture exited the place. She placed the rifle next to the shotgun, loosened the rope from the hitching post, and straddled her pony. Soon she was off to track the visitor, who followed the man.

She rode faster than either of the two parties that left the trading post earlier. Her horse, better equipped for cutting in and out of the bayou, made better speed than a bunch of pilgrims on a leisure path through the bayou to head west. Soon she could see the back of the stagecoach, and slowed to the coach's pace, following it. Something eerie about the situation bugged her, but she did not know why.

Rumors had circulated around the Red River about families traveling West across the Bayou disappearing, but this was Louisiana, myths and tales get tossed around like the prostitutes in New Orleans brothels. No one knew if these rumors were true. Sara sped up the horse, erasing the distance between her and the family. The wagon approached a clearing about a few hundred yards wide. On it was a small farm that looked uninhabited at first, with overgrown vegetation, and fields in need of harvesting and the bushes surrounding the house in dire need of some trimming. Sara stopped the horse and raised her field glasses to watch.

The sun descended over the Texas sky, sitting to the West from where she rode. Sara grabbed the reins and pushed forward; she still had a few hundred yards in the bayou. Soon the young woman neared a clearing where no one could spot her, but still she made out the surroundings without the glasses. She watched the clan pull the coach adjacent to the farm.

A man resembling the same man she saw leaving the merchant's shop exited the front door and started talking to the father, the driver of the stage. He got off as the man took the stage around to the back. After a minute or two, Sara noticed the mother and children run towards the door. The man must have let them spend the night. After all, the group appeared to have a long journey, and Sara guessed they needed a bunk for the night, and she retreated further into the bayou.

Sara started a small campfire, set up some traps, and stretched out her bedroll across the mud. She caught a couple of rabbits, skinned and kept the carcass, and cleaned the meat. Soon, she cooked the bunnies up on the flame. After a snort of the whiskey, she had a bowl of the Perique from her pipe, pulled the hat down over her eyes and drifted off to sleep.

Chapter 6

The blood-curdling screams woke her up. Ear piercing and coming from the west, from the clearing in the bayou. Sara wiped the dust from her eyes, pulled her field glasses to her eyes, but saw no one. The wagon was gone, no one was around. She stayed watching the house. It was a wooden frame small house with an angled roof. It looked well made and had a barn in the back, which she could see as she snuck up in the trees to get a better look. Still no sign of the Pilgrims as she searched past the home. Maybe there was another path, or they cut through the bayou. It was time to sneak up and get a better look. She filled her vest with shells, mounted her horse, tapped the steed with her heels so it moved slow, and headed to the minute plantation home.

Girl and horse crept up, meandering between the trees. She carried the shotgun in her right hand, leaving the left to grip the reins, guiding the horse towards the clearing. They stayed behind the tree line as long as possible. She stopped the pony before the last set of trees. Soon she would be in the clearing. She peered through the glasses in search of the pioneers. Nothing, not even movement from the house. She wondered where the scream had emerged from. It sounded human, but it could have been a critter caught in a trap. Her heart quickened. Beads of sweat cascaded from her hairline. With the horse sitting still, she wiped her face dry with the back of her hand. She closed her eyes, took deep breaths to relax herself before commencing into full outlaw mode.

She grabbed the reins tight, kicked the steed, and the horse galloped from the bayou into the clearing, down the path towards the house. They sped past it in search of the Sabine River. It was a good day's ride for a stage, and they would have to bunk up there before crossing.

She did not know why she was curious about this family. Maybe because her family was butchered and consequently raised by strangers. The Native family that took her in was a hybrid family. Mothers and children vanished towards the nations, while her ancestors were bought and sold throughout the South. She rode hard across the Western Louisiana bayou, crossing the prairie grasses and winded through the pecan trees. Her hope of catching up with the family faltered, as she still found no sight of them.

Arriving at an abandoned fort, she paused, realizing that neither she nor the horse had time for a drink and some food. She crept into the bayou and tied up her still nameless steed before venturing to capture some food. She laid traps, then set off to gather water in a nearby creek. The horse ate some grass and leaves, taking its time to slurp up water from the stream, exhausted from having worked hard to getting Sara this far. Sara found some berries, returned to the traps, and extracted a couple of rabbits. Done eating, she relaxed with her pipe and some Perique tobacco, puffing on it. She thought about a snort of whiskey as well, grabbed the bottle, opened it, and took a small sip. She squinted, spat it out, and took another shot.

After returning the bottle to her roll and dumping the burnt tobacco into the fire, she doused the flames. Her ears perked up to a sound in the distance. Silently, she crawled on all fours behind a row of pecan trees.

"I know you're there." Came a voice towards the east of her. "Come out with your hands up." She had done nothing wrong. With Sara's gun cocked and aimed towards the man's voice. "Whoever you are, whether you're one of them freed niggers or a renegade injun, we don't want you here. Ya hear me?"

She stayed put for a second, hoping the voice would reveal his location, and peaked around, looking for more shelter. She fired off two rounds into the trees, reloaded the shotgun, and sprinted towards the next tree line.

"Ah, you're closer than I thought," the voice resumed, much   closer.
Sara guessed the man was about fifty yards from her. She crept up, heading east behind the trees and crawling through the snake enhanced mud. Her eyes fixed on a king snake, she crept up to the man, who inched his way towards where Sara hid. A shot rang out and ricochet off a tree towards her south.

"They been killing some innocent people around here. There's a bounty out for da killer, and I think I found him. Come   on   out.   I   might   not   shoot   ya."
His rifle aimed in her direction. Sara grabbed two more shells from her vest, set them in the dirt beside her. She eyed the snake and then the man, unsure if this be self-defense. He shot at her first.

"You making me mad there. I know ya da killer. These are innocent peoples here, just folks passing through. Come out with your hands up." She got a good look at him as he snuck towards where she once hid. He was a large man, fat, with gray hair and a full gray beard. He stood about twenty-five yards from her. She had a clear shot. She fired both shells and replaced them as fast as she emptied the barrel. The man turned to shoot, but he was too late. Sara Barnum took her first life. He laid in a pool of blood.

The man, a bounty hunter, former confederate soldier and former slave hunter, meant nothing to Sara. He still had a wife waiting for his return and five children. Jobs were scarce during reconstruction.

A man did what he had to do; rumors spread about families disappearing in this area. He tracked the wrong person and got sloppy about it.

Sara looked around. Not seeing anyone, she grabbed the man's rifle and ammo and left him. The wildlife needed to eat as gators walked across the bayou, and one of the beasts could have a feast with the dead fat man. She continued towards the Sabine in search of the clan. She wanted to know if they ferried across the raging waters, or if they were among the missing, which the deceased bounty hunter searched for.

Sara shook like pecan trees during a storm as she mounted her steed. She kicked it a little harder than she should, and the horse took off towards the river. Upset by the hour delay, the two-rode hard. They became one as Sara streamlined her position as she lowered her head as the westerly winds blew in from Texas. She made the Sabine at about four o'clock, since they took the most direct route. Then she scouted the riverfront for a ferry.

Riding north, she spied two men with the appearance of old veterans from the war with a raft meant to carry people across the river. They sat under a cypress, smoking a pipe and sharing a bottle of whiskey. Sara trotted towards them, doubting they even heard the earlier shooting.

"Howdy, youngster," the younger of the two greeted, dressed in a gray confederate uniform with torn sleeves and ripped pants. The cap he wore begged for a good sew job. The older, larger, and stronger man sat in ragged overalls that needed some tailor work, took snort after snort of whiskey, and didn't even look up. "You need a ride across the river?" the younger man asked. "We could use some business. Ain't no one been here all day."

Sara's legs shook, her breath heavier than normal. She alighted from her horse, grateful for an opportunity to stretch her legs. Her whiskey soon came flying out. She took a quick sip to calm her nerves, then grabbed a plug of tobacco, stuffing the plugs in her pipe. She lit it and took a large puff, exhaling the smoke into the Louisiana sky.

"Is this the only ferry in the area?" She attempted to man-up her voice, speaking in deeper tones, but failed.

The younger man looked at her. "Well, ma'am, this is the only one for miles. You want to go to Texas, you got to ride with us, and we'd be more than happy to get you across the river." He kicked his partner with his pointed boots. The boots torn as well. "Lookie here, Zeke, we got us a young lass out on her own. She might be one of them freed girls, too."

The other man smiled at her. It wasn't cordial. Spittle formed at the side of his mouth.

"We be more than happy to give you a ride across da river." He panted, watching the young girl with a fixed stare.

The other man strolled towards her, hand on his pistol. Sara was at close range; two men, two shells, making it easy to rid these two if needed. "Nah, I don't want to go over there. Just wondering about the ferries, but much obliged." She tipped her hat, the act causing her long dark hair to tumble out.

"Oh, you a mighty fine-looking thing," the younger man said. "We are taking you across the river. Might even give you a free ride." He reached for his revolver in his hip holster.

"Thanks anyway, but I need to head back to town. People are expecting me, so I gotta get moving." She turned towards the horse but stopped at the click of a revolver. "I say you coming with us. I can tell you a little half-breed bitch. We are taking you for a river ride. You stop right there and come with us." He spat a wad of tobacco on the ground.

Sara turned around to face two guns pointed at her. She wasn't going anywhere with these two gentlemen. Two men, two shells, two shots, she thought to herself.

"I need to get my horse and gear if I go with you" she turned back and started walking.

"You stop right there. You don't need nothing else but what you got on your back. Just drop that shotgun." She spun around and saw his finger on the trigger, but his hand shook. The other man struggled to relight a pipe, his gun resting on the ground beside him.

The gun-waving man had trouble aiming. He'd miss if he fired, but she hesitated to take that chance.

"I said drop that shot gun or I'll shoot you right now."

"You ain't gonna shoot me. You got no reason to. If you shoot me, you can't rape me, and that's what you want." She tightened her grip on the gun, pointed it at the man, and pulled one trigger. He fell back. She raised it to her eyes as the other man struggled to pick up his gun. He never made it. He laid in a crimson pool of crimson; his stationery arm inches from his firearm. "More gator food," she said, mounting her horse, galloping off.

Three men left for dead in one afternoon. Maybe there were three widows waiting with dinner for them to come home. Maybe there were several children waiting for their Pa's return. She pressed down on the guilt. All three had weapons. They either fired at her or attempted to. One of them suggested a rape and river swim. She rode off to seek shelter in the bayou. Someone would report the two confederate veterans missing. Sara would not be around. She cut through the bayou on horseback with no direction.

Chapter 7

"It was good for our fathers, it was good for our fathers, it's good enough for me. Gimme that old time religion, gimme that old time religion, gimme that old time religion, it's good enough for me, "the young girl sang, walking behind her family out of the old Georgia church on Sunday. The townspeople wished them well as they departed church that Sunday. Rose's family needed to finish packing the remainder of their belongings in the covered wagon.

Rose strolled towards the wagon, adding the second, third and fourth verse to the song, while her father spoke with the folks he'd be missing. "Damn scalawags, anyway, coming down infiltrating our way of life. Let them freedman come back and own our land. Hell, my brother went on up and left, followed the Cherokee, and living in freedom in the Indian Nations. We be out to live with them."

"Ya don't say," the reverend said. "Well, I ought to say a prayer for you, then." He looked around, caught sight of Rose humming a few verses, and hollered at her. "You mosey on over here," the preacher called out after the lass, not afraid to give her a whooping if she didn't come over. Baptist preachers in 1886 Savannah cared less.

The man in cloth gave her his look when the youngest child of Samuel Dunning acted like an eight-year-old. Rose hurried over to stand in the shadows of the church. The white steeple stood above the town; the spire seeming to be the highest point in the coastal town. They stood in a circle. She grabbed on to her father with one hand, and the other took hold of her older sister's hand, while her sister grasped her brother's hand. The sixteen-year-old only son didn't want to travel. He disagreed with his father about the infiltration of the carpetbaggers in the coastal city. He sought to seek reform, but Mr. Dunning, always was handy with a switch, was persuasive.

The brother clung to his mother's hand, who grasped the preacher's, who held hands with both the father and mother. The circle tight, preventing the devil from entering. They bowed, hands clenched to one another, forming an unbreakable chain.

The Preacher started reading. "I will quote Exodus 17.1 for your journey. *And all the congregation of the children of Israel journeyed from the wilderness of Sin, after their journeys, according to the commandment of the Lord, and pitched in Rephidim: and there was no water for the people to drink.*"

2. "Wherefore the people did chide with Moses, and said, give us water that we may drink. And Moses said unto them, why chide ye with me? Wherefore do ye tempt the Lord?"

3. "And the people thirsted there for water; and the people murmured against Moses, and said, wherefore is this that thou hast brought us up out of Egypt, to kill us and our children and our cattle with thirst?

4. And Moses cried unto the Lord, saying, what shall I do unto this people? they be almost ready to stone me.

.5 And the Lord said unto Moses, go on before the people, and take with thee of the elders of Israel; and thy rod, wherewith thou smites the river, take in thine hand, and go.

6.Behold, I will stand before thee there upon the rock in Horeb; and thou shalt smite the rock, and there shall come water out of it, that the people may drink. And Moses did so in the sight of the elders of Israel.

7.And he called the name of the place Massah, and Meribah, because of the chiding of the children of Israel, and because they tempted the Lord, saying, Is the Lord among us, or not?

8. Then came Amalek and fought with Israel in Rephidim.

9.And Moses said unto Joshua, choose us out men, and go out, fight with Amalek: tomorrow I will stand on the top of the hill with the rod of God in mine hand. Amen."

The family repeated Amen in unison. Rose sprinted towards their carriage. It would be her last ride in it. Soon she would ride in the back of a covered wagon. The rest of the clan shook the preacher's hand and caught up with Rose. They rode home, bouncing down the road out past the town limit to their small farm. After their last Sunday dinner at home, they finished packing their entire life in the covered wagon.

The next morning, the covered wagon sat packed full. The Dunnings left way too much behind to start their new life. They left no sprawling room in the wagon. The clan ventured west. The journey would be long, over two months, but Samuel Dunning craved departing the New South. Reconstruction was not his way of life. Scalawags infiltrated Savannah, and Mr. Dunning hurried his kin out the door. The journey slid uneventful. Mr. Dunning took the ropes with his wife beside him and the boy beside her. Rose and her sister sat in back with their belongings.

Times throughout the trip, the children, mother and father alternated walking beside the wagon, giving the horses a break from the weight and slowing them down. Crossing the Appalachians slowed them down while their steeds crawled up the mountains and went down. Once past on the other side of Georgia, they cruised and arrived at the great river in about one month. The Mississippi.

The sun stood straight above, though they bunked for the night near in Vicksburg.

Mr. Dunning walked around town, speaking to his wife and children. "This is where we lost the war. We lost everything, our entire land, right here. Damn Yankees split the army in half by taking the town. I think we should all close our eyes and bow our heads in silence." The family gathered, holding hands in their unyielding bond. Rose opened her eyes, peeking, holding on to her brother's hand. His eyes opened, head turned back, peering across the state of Mississippi. He glanced down, caught Rose's glare, and they both smirked. They clasped their hands tighter, closing their eyes and bowed their heads. Soon, the Dunnings bounced into town in the packed covered wagon to get a nice bite to eat from a café and bunk down in a shady hotel.

Tired legs, tired bottoms, they spent an extra day. The horses drooped their heads in fatigue. However, the family needed to move on, since all were tired. The route they took may have been longer, but the Southern route across Dixie appeared the most logical to mountainous terrain.

All packed, they waited on the ferry, staring out across the mass river.

"That river is so wide. You can barely see across it." Rose shouted to her kin, hand above her eyes like she saluted Robert E. Lee. Her blonde braids descended past her shoulders, covered by a yellow bonnet. "It's like the ocean."

Her parents and older sibling giggled at the youngest Dunning, all waiting for Samuel to be done paying the ferry operator. Soon all were on board the ferry boat, which struggled with the current of the mighty river. It did not take long to arrive in the West, and in the great state of Louisiana. Trudging through the swamps of Louisiana, it took a week to cross the state. The Dunnings slowed their journey near a bayou. Lost in a swamp with alligators, snakes and cypress trees, their journey delayed in the Central part of the state. The Kisatchie forest, thick with Cypress and pecan trees, shifted the family's direction.

Exiting the area, their wagon scooted through the valley, intent on making the Sabine River at the edge of the state, still a couple of days out. Supplies ran low. At about the time they were tired, hungry and exhausted in the clearing, they noticed a trading post outside of a small town, flanked by a thick bayou. Mr. Dunning studied the map. He announced they had lost their direction because of their tribulation through the Kisatchie Forest. Left with no choice, the family trudged through the long and thick savannah grass. They exited the bayou, frazzled by the humidity, heat, and the ghosts of the bayou.

Someone spied on them through her field glasses. Sara Barnum focused on the Georgians. She watched them disperse water amongst family members through their canteens. All the family but the mother who led the team walked beside the wagon, reducing the workload for the exhausted horses. One time, Sara noticed the little blonde girl sit in the mud, but her siblings grabbed each arm, lifting her to her feet, while the young girl with the long blonde braids struggled to stand. They lifted her into the wagon, so she stretched out in the crowded back, allowing the family to progress west.

Sara squatted deeper in the grass. At one point, the girl on the back of the covered wagon turned her head to stare at Sara as she disappeared further in the forest. The girl remained peering in Sara's direction while the wagon bounced through the tall grass. Sara Barnum closed her eyes. She got a well-deserved fifteen-minute nap at about the time it took the wagon to pass. They stopped in the market, seizing the opportunity to stretch their legs and purchase supplies for the next leg of their journey. The father, tall and eloquent, dressed in a dark suit, wore a stove-top hat reminiscent of President Lincoln. Beside him, the mother wore a long dark skirt, white blouse, and topped her head with a flowered bonnet.

The three children, aged from about eight to thirteen, ran around in circles before entering the establishment with their parents. They left the dog outside the covered wagon.

A man followed the travelers into the store. Sara watched him from afar, her field glasses resting on her nose. The scene seemed familiar. A clan traveling west, an elusive man, and she hid in the Pecan trees to watch. Weeks earlier, the same scenario, with three men dead and the girl on the run. She focused in on the man, who seemed to be the same man as before.

Sara crept up on her faithful steed. They rested behind the store, long enough for Sara to remove herself from the horse. In jeans, a denim shirt and her hat pulled down to cover her face, she snuck up, searching for a window for a peep inside the establishment. Still carrying her double barrel, she crept towards the front door, glancing around.

The voices were inside and in-between the kids' scream, Sara made out a woman's voice and three men. She kept near the wall, pacing herself, eyes bouncing around. She eyed a poster hanging on the front door. A wanted poster with a reward for five-hundred dollars under a picture of a young woman. She studied the rough sketch of a female with a flattened hat and smiled. She was wanted for the disappearance of a family, and the murder of three men. The ferry operators, and the bounty hunter. She stayed put for a moment, eavesdropping.

"It's pretty safe travel out there," a voice she assumed as belonging to the attendant was speaking to the Georgia travelers. "There's some renegade half-breed out there, heading west. Doubt if she came back here after the trail of blood she left. I think she headed to Texas."

"Well, we be headed through there. Need to make the Injun territories. We got to head west, but we looking for a place to bunk down for a couple of days."

"Well folks, I got me a house down yonder not too far from here. It's a couple miles down the path here. My wife and I are more than welcome you for a few days. I'm sure that girl is long gone, anyway. Best way is to let her get space between us."

Sara considered hiding, yet her suspicion of the man grew at an alarming pace. She edged forward, intending to check out the house again. She wondered if this man performed the killings and was responsible for the missing families crossing the bayou. The shop keeper, the entrepreneur that could identify her. As far as she knew, he was the sole person who spotted her. Was he in on it as well? Were there any other families passing through that never made it across the river? There wasn't a ferry service unless a couple of other job seekers stole the ferrying business from the dead men.

She mounted the horse and galloped towards the house through the bayou. She needed to scout it out. No longer able to return to the trading post, she would be on her own.

From behind the pecan trees, Sara scouted out the house. She hid only one hundred yards from the residence, granting her a perfect view of the house, from where the barn appeared even grander. Her horse tied up, her bedroll opened, she waited.

She set traps for some rabbits, possum, racoons, or squirrels, anything she could nab for food, furs or anything she needed. She required becoming self-sufficient and everything she trapped or shot required being used. Anything else left could be clues to her whereabouts. At least, the people assumed she departed Louisiana.

She spied the mam ride up on his steed. He got off the horse and went into the barn, probably slipped in to clean up for his kinfolk. Maybe he got rid of some previous deceased bodies. Sara peered towards the east and noticed the Conestoga Wagon approaching. She kept her eye on it, creeping back further into the swamp.

She cleaned the rabbits she caught, stripped the fur off the critters, grilled them on the small fire she built in the backwoods, and had a dinner of hare and berries. She took a shot of whiskey, smoked her pipe, and slept next to the smoldering embers of her small fire.

Sara spent the next two nights hiding out in the bayou, a watchful eye on the barn during the day. At night, she sat staring at the sky, as she felt safe snuggled amongst the trees, not worrying about the slithering reptiles sneaking around. She was one with them and knew which ones were poisonous and which varmints were harmless. She was at ease with the large reptilian alligators that strolled along the bayou and knew how to handle them if needed. Sara Barnum, a warrior for all, learned her craft from the Caddo.

She never heard the rustling of the leaves as tiny footsteps approached her. "Hey you." The voice was of a young girl.

"Are you sleeping over there?" Sara reached for the shotgun.

"Why are you getting your gun?" Sara brushed her eyes, rising with her firearm.

"Why are you here? What are you doing?" The voice got louder as its owner approached.

Pointing the shotgun to the ground, Sara replied, "Watcha doing back here? This ain't no place for a little kid." She strolled towards the child's voice, creeping behind the pecan and cypress trees, careful not to be spotted.

"I think I'm lost." Her tiny voice didn't sound panicked. Sara tightened the grip on the gun. "I can't find my way around here with all these trees. Can you help me?" The squeaky voice approached, not more than twenty yards away.

Sara wanted to help, but common sense yelled at her to pack quick and take off. Her luck was on the shoulders of an impressionable toddler. Toddlers could be manipulated, and the girl might have seen the wanted poster. She might be the traveler' kids, and she couldn't take any chances. Still, there were creatures back here in the bayou that would snap up the young girl if she wasn't smart.

This kid sounded like a toddler would when exploring a bayou. Precious, curious, and naïve, lead to gator bait. Sara crept up, sheltering in the bayou, doing her best to remain hidden. She edged closer to where the voice rang out. "Ma'am, who are you?" the little girl called out. "Answer me. I'm getting scared." The voice resonated in panic. "Answer me, please."

Sara soon stood in the clearing. The girl stood in an open area, not more than ten yards from Sara. She wore a long dress, her blonde hair braided. Her body trembled. "Ah!" the girl screamed as Sara raised a finger to her own lips to quiet the young girl.

"Hey, little girl. This bayou ain't the right place for a kid." Sara crept up, a forceful grip on the gun.

The girl sprinted up to her. "Can you help me? I'm not from here. We're staying with a family down over on a farm for the last few days. I don't know their name and I took a walk in here, since the trees are so pretty, and I got lost. I need to find my way back. She shook when she talked. Her hands pointed at the dugout cypress trees in the bayou, as well as towards the clearing. Sara hugged her.

"Yeah, I'll get you back to the clearing. Don't tell no one you went walking out here."

"Why? It's real pretty down here. We're from Georgia, heading towards the Indian Nations. Are we close to them?"

"The Nations are a pretty big place, civilized tribes there. I might have some old kin up there."

"I'm with my ma and pa, and my brother and sister. We are staying with my dad's brother. He fought in the war. Did your daddy fight in the war?" She spoke with a sweet Southern accent.

"Yeah, he did. Yanks shot him down not too far from here. That's why I hang out here. I never met him and only heard stories about him. Staying out here makes me feel close to him."

"Daddy told me his brother ran off. Didn't want to shoot no one anymore. Wasn't even sure why they were fighting."

Both girls started walking towards the clearing. In the distance, they heard a faint scream, like someone calling a name. It might have been a scream of fear. Sara held the girl back for a minute. The minute turned longer, long enough for the kid to cling to her leg, shaking like the tropical storms that passed through each autumn.

At the edge of the clearing, they heard noises similar to howling dragons circling in the bayou, as gators bellowed, and bullfrogs croaked, the noises deafening. "Something happened." Sara said, pulling the child to retreat towards the bayou.

"Someone calling you?" Sara asked the youngster.

"I can't tell."

"Was that your ma or pa's voice calling out?"

"I don't know what they sound like."

Sara stared at the girl. She attempted a smile to make the child warm up to her. It didn't work.

The shaking girl grabbed Sara's leg tighter. "It, it, it did... didn't sound like it," she stuttered.

Sara glanced down at the girl, and then towards her horse. She wasn't about to let this child wander to the house alone, or alone in the bayou. This was a girl from the hills and would be a snack for some of these creatures wandering through their reptilian home swamp.

The law wanted Sara, as they plastered her face on the doors and windows of the trading post, and who knew where else her image was portrayed.

"We're gonna ride up, check things out. First thing is we have to pack up the camp. If everything is good, I'll drop you off, but I gotta ride away. Mention nothing if your ma and pa are okay. Do you understand me?"

The girl stared at her in silence, still shaking in rhythm with the pecan trees. Sara held her tight, guiding her towards the steed. They gathered up her gear, rolled her bedroll up nice and tight, and placed it on the back of the horse. Sara lifted the girl up, settling her in front of the bedroll.

"Sit there and don't move. Hang on tight to me while we ride."

Sara loaded up a rifle and her shotgun, her vest packed full of ammunition. If the rumors about families disappearing were true, she knew who was responsible. She wondered if this precious girl was an orphan at a similar age that she became one.

They trotted, at first meandering around the tall trees. They approached the clearing, riding even slower, listening for any voices. Sara stopped the horse frequently to glance at the house, then the barn. When they reached the clearing, they had a non-obstructed view. On finding nothing, she figured it was time to check out the home, the barn, search for a covered wagon and any sign of body dismemberment.

"Wrap your arms around my stomach as tight as you can. We're gonna ride as fast as this horse can take us."

The youngster gripped Sara as tight as her little arms could, clenching her hands together over Sara's belly. "I... I, I am scared now."

"It's okay." Sara tried to reassure her. She was shaking as well but tried to act calm in this situation. She had taken lives before and wasn't afraid to shoot again if needed.

A kick in the belly sent the horse galloping towards the barn. With one eye on the house, another on the barn, they arrived in a matter of minutes. Still, they saw nothing out of the ordinary. The door that led into the house remained closed, the barn doors shut tight with no livestock or humans in sight.

Thirty minutes ago, there was screaming. If parents were calling for Rose, they'd be searching the grounds looking for her. Sara circled around the land. The horse trotted as she peered for movement.

Her last resort was to figure out how to open the barn and search inside the building. The girl relaxed her grip on Sara as they trotted up. Sara turned to the girl. "I'm jumping off, so you need to let go."

The girl refused at first, but finally relaxed her grip on Sara. Sara turned the horse around so she could board the horse from the left to make a quick escape if required. The door remained locked tight with a padlock. She grabbed her rifle and fired at the lock, blowing it in shambles. Unlatching the door, she pried it open. No wagon, no family sleeping, no belongings.

Sara looked up at the girl. "Isn't this where you were staying? Weren't you sleeping in the barn for a few days?"

Moisture dripped down the girl's face. She nodded her. Sara mounted the horse. The parents wouldn't leave without their youngest. "Hang on as tight as you can." The girl gripped Sara tighter than before. Sara gouged the horse with her heels, and the animal raced off towards the bayou.

"There she is. That's the killer," a male voice rang out behind   them.

Shots whizzed by. Soon they were in the forest, meandering through pecan trees. Sara rode past where she set up camp. A few miles of northbound riding, they approached another clearing where an abandoned slave cabin sat. Off in the distance, she saw a home that appeared to be left alone. A building next to it lay in ashes. It might have been a casualty of the war since Yankee troops took their liberty on Confederate property.

"Let's check this out. We need some shelter." Sara halted the horse, staring at the dark sky. It appeared night had fallen, but it was slightly past noon. "We'll have to head out quick as soon as we get some grub in our bellies. Once this storm passes, I reckon they will be looking for us, and this will be the first place they will check."

Sara pushed in the door to the cabin. From the floors that laid caked in mud, a king snake slithered out, followed by two more.

"I hate snakes," Rose shrieked in alarm, instinctively clinging on to Sara. "When can we get to my uncles?"

"Depends on where he lives over there. It's an enormous area. Watcha daddy say about it?"

"I don't know, but I think he said another month." She stared at Sara with those innocent blue eyes.

Sara smiled. "We should make it in less than that, but we need to check it out. There will be people looking for us. I'll have to check things out before we cross. Might have to make a stop or two, hold out for a bit. I know us a place to stay."

The little girl sat down. With no belongings, no toys, no change of clothes with her, she would need a couple of new dresses, or at least a pair of jeans to wear, and something to cover her pretty hair and head from the searing sun. There was no sun as Sara glanced out the window. It was dark as night, but the rains hadn't commenced, but it was a matter of time.

Soon, the tin roof of the former slave cabin sounded like a drummer marching across the shack, playing their instruments. The rat-a-tat pounded harder and harder. It sounded like a steam train coming through as the winds picked up. The dark skies turned green; a twister was nearby. Sara motioned Rose to get to the southwest corner of the cabin and get as low as possible. She laid on top of the girl, protecting her precious life with her own.

She closed her eyes, whispering so Rose couldn't hear her, "Whoever is out there, please protect us. I know someone is out there listening and I'll get gifts if you need them. I remember my Mama gave you some things to protect us. Please protect me and this child if you can hear me."

Rose got lost in her own brief prayer. "Dear Jesus, please protect me and my new friend. I'm scared. Keep us safe through this storm. Amen."

The storm passed, leaving the shack intact, however water came through the roof and broke out windows. Puddles piled on the mud floors like little ponds. Sara appeared like she had taken a bath, while Rose sprawled out on the floor caked in mud. Even though they were drenched, dirty and terrified, they remained safe since someone protected them.

Sara walked over to the window to peek outside. She noticed trees fell like they were victims of the nearby sawmill. The burned-out tiny plantation home had split in half with the walls collapsed. Sara had earlier had an inkling to stay in that place, but reconsidered, after figuring that would be the first building any chasers would search. The horse, nervous, whinnied several times, pacing around the cabin.

"I doubt if I can start a fire yet. The ground is soaked." Sara snuck outside the cabin. "I got some grub packed away in my pack here. It's berries and jerky. Ain't nothing fancy, but it will have to do. I still got this canteen of water, but we gotta save a little until I can refill. Can't drink the groundwater, but we will if we have to."

Rose nibbled on pieces of jerky, sipped from one of Sara's canteens, and snacked on some of the fresh berries Sara picked over the last two days. "This is good." She smiled at Sara. "I wish we could have some biscuits or some stew, but this is good for now."

"I promise you, I'll make us a delicious stew when the time comes. Right now, we gotta eat fast, ride quick. I know us a little place where we can stock up, rest and hide out before we head west. We are going there in a bit. I need to rest my stinky dogs." She tossed her boots and stretched out her toes.

Chapter 8

The sun came out after an hour's darkness. Rose helped more than she hindered the trip by helping Sara gather the belonging. Sara led the mudder of a horse outside the cabin and helped Rose onto the steed's back. Sara mounted the pony, and they trotted off, Rose once again clenching onto Sara's belly. They galloped North, slicing through the trees, careful of the fallen ones that blocked the trails. Only feeling safe after they got through the storm damage. They trotted along the trail, making decent speed towards the river. They headed towards the little Indian village, where the natives could nurture Little Rose until Sara concluded it was safe to venture across Texas and to the Nations.

Sara sought shelter along the way. She kept an eye out for sharecropping cabins, former slave quarters, burnt out homes they could sleep in, and to protect the little girl from wild critters rambling through the bayous, plus any sudden storms appearing in the evening. The war was over for about twenty years, reconstruction was happening, there were plenty of places to stay. Louisiana and the rest of the South was sprinkled with them.

Sara passed a few on the way, and when they approached a clearing, they galloped through the opening of the bayou past villages, farms and plantations until reaching the forest, where they zigzagged through the thick trees. Getting close to sunset, she found a little burnt-out cabin near the stream, where they dismounted and headed inside.

Sara made a fire over which she boiled some water from the brook. Then she took out her rifle, shot some rabbits, and picked more blackberries. After dinner, they bunked for the night. Voices filtering in the night air woke Rose up. She didn't recognize them, probably flunky bounty hunters. They weren't the family she stayed with.

Sara put her finger to her lips. "Shh," she whispered to her young companion. She flicked her hand, motioning Rose to return to the back of the shack. Her pony lifted its head, peering around. She grabbed a handful of berries, paced towards the steed. One hand containing berries opened to feed her ride. She petted the animal with the other, rubbing its head. She spoke in a soft tone, relaxing the beast. Her glance lingered to Rose sitting in the corner, still shaking. "I'll be there in a sec."

"They got to be near," a voice echoed out. "What about that lil old-abandoned shanty over there?" The voice had a deeper pitch.

Rose's ears perked up, recognizing the voice. She attempted to speak, but nerves squelched her voice. Sara moseyed across the shack. She grabbed her shotgun, checked it to make sure the gun remained loaded. "Did you recognize that voice?"

Rose stuttered. "I, I, I think so." She looked scared out of her   wits. Sara pointed the gun at the front door, unsure if they'd come in. She hoped they rode past, but part of her hoped they'd barge in. An explosive welcome awaited the trespassers.

The voices became louder.

"Shh," the voice Rose recognized told the other one. "If they're here, we don't want them to know." The man slurred a little. He sounded drunk, his whisper resonating louder than his partner's.

The shotgun was ready, pointed at the door, and Sara expected two more notches on her belt.

"Get your pistol ready, just in case," the initial voice said. "Reward money for the woman, while the kid can reunite with her parents."

"I told you to whisper," the recognized voice came louder than before. They sounded near the entrance. "If they're here, they can hear us."

"I'm the damn sheriff in this parish. I might know that young lady as well. Open the door and fire when I say. We want her dead."

Silence followed, except for the creaking of the door. Sara caught movements through the moonlight reflection on the broken-out windows. The horse whinnied as the door flew open.

Sara pulled the first trigger, and the second followed instantly. The men never got a shot off. Sara motioned Rose to remain seated in the corner. She rushed towards the door, shotgun in hand. Through the shadows, she saw two bodies sprawled on the ground. They appeared lifeless on their backs. Not taking any chances, she emptied her weapon into them. Two more murders. One was a sheriff. She sprinted over to Rose, aided her on the horse. Rushing back in, she gathered their belongings in a bedroll, and placed it on her faithful animal. Hurriedly mounting the steed, they rode out of the shanty into a dark bayou. She guided the horse, meandering through the bayou, mud splashing upon the animal and themselves, and they rode until they hit a clearing. It must have been hours. Sara, oblivious to their location, decided it was best to bunk out. With the bayou behind them, they slept on the edge of the forest. She sought the Red River, knowing she could follow it to the mini reservation.

Neither slept. Sara spent her time admiring the innocence of the youngster, who tossed and turned on the soggy bottom. The young woman remembered being eight years old herself, and witnessing a town of innocent people slaughtered, while the state called it a riot.

"Would this sweet, innocent child turn into an outlaw? Would she shoot first, ask questions later? Not if I have anything to do with it." Sara pondered. She stayed up all night, staring at the kid.

As the sun peeked over the eastern skies, she crawled through the brush to survey the area. Folks riding horses and wagons bounced along paths, including colored folks headed to the market in carts drug by mules. All signs that a community must be close. She snuck back to their camp-out to begin a small fire, grabbed her shotgun, and sent a couple of rabbits bouncing dead. After berry hunting, they had a breakfast of rabbit and blackberries before she crawled out to further scope the area. The path seemed more occupied with horse and buggies; mule driven carts packed on the path.

"Rose, come here. Stay low."

Rose crawled over in her mud-caked clothes, peering out across the clearing. "Do you think we can blend in with the travelers? We can ride beside them as if nothing happened."

Rose looked at her like she was crazy. She still shook, but Sara understood why. The girl, in the last few days, witnessed her parents' murder. She witnessed her savior blowing two men away, one a self-described lawman, and not ceasing with one shot. Sara had continued the execution further past their last breath.

"I want to stay here. I'm afraid to go anywhere."

"I think we're safe now," Sara insisted. "We will blend in. Plus, I know a place we can hide out for a bit." She looked at Rose, then glanced back at the landscape. "Yeah, we might be a day's ride trotting." She stomped past the girl, feet squishing in the wet soil. "Let's wait a bit until it's all clear and we should ride out and get on the path."

Sara aided a resisting Rose on the horse. The young girl kicked her legs, but Sara clung on to her with a hug, reassuring her that everything was fine. She plopped the youngster on the back, in front of the saddlebag, leading the pony to a clearing from where she mounted her beast, and rode off towards the path, galloping north.

They rode slowly, as if on a leisure ride. Sara tipped her hat to the riders heading south in their buggies, wagons, or carts, smiling at them. The sun shone bright, as it approached its apex, Sara recognized their surroundings.

"Let's take a break here. Sneak off into them trees over yonder. They be right by the river. We can ride up the riverbank, and I know these folks who will protect us for a bit."

They stopped short of the flowing water, carefully making their way through the rocky shore. The horse stuck its face in the water, lapping the liquid and quenching his thirst. Sara and Rose took a walk to stretch their legs. They admired the shoreline from across the river. Trees lined up next to the shore, while the water looked a little murky from the recent storms.

Rose glanced at Sara after stretching her arms high above her head. "Sure is pretty here. So, who we gonna stay with?"

"I know some Caddo. They raised me since I was eleven and live not too far from here. We can sneak up here along the river. I know the back-way in." Sara smiled at the kid, acting confident in her journey.

"Are the Caddo Indians? Daddy warned us of Indian attacks on the way." Rose's body still shook. Her eyes widened.

"Yeah, they're Indians, but peaceful. I learnt a lot from them about how to survive. I gotcha out of that situation back there, didn't I?"

"Yeah, but you had to shoot people?"

"Well, something I learned from my people before living with da Caddo, kill or be killed. I don't wanna die. I got me a job to do, and that's getting you to your kinfolk." They continued their stroll along the river. Both young ladies tossed stones into the water and watched the flat pebbles splash and circles abound from the point of entry. Sara grabbed a flat one, threw it side-armed into the river, and they watched it skip a few times across the water.

"I want to try."

"Okay, Rose, let's find you a perfect one."

They bent over, searching for hand-sized flat rocks to skip. Sara separated from Rose in her search. She bent down, tossed a couple aside, and squealed as they plopped into the river. She grabbed a few more rocks, generously handing a couple to Rose. "Here you go."

Rose attempted to throw overhand.

"No, no, not that way. You need to throw with your arm at the side. Let me show you." Sara grabbed her arm from behind, pulling it straight horizontal. "Now flick, and see what happens."

Rose tossed. It splashed once into the river. Sara handed her another stone and Rose improved this time around. It skipped three times, and the final toss skipped five. Rose looked up and smiled.

"Thank you, Sara. You're an excellent teacher."

Sara pointed upriver. "See that patch of trees up there? Those are pecan trees. The Caddo should be on the other side. Let's mosey on up there."

"Can we throw some more rocks?"

"Yeah. Grab some, make sure they're flat. Flat ones are the best."

The two girls spent another half hour pillaging the river's edge for flat stones, attempting to skip them across the muddy stream. Rose hit seven for her personal best, while Sara topped out at six.

Rose gloated over being the winner.

"Of course, you're a winner. Let's ride up."

Rose smiled as Sara aided her on. As soon as Sara mounted, they trotted up the river towards the Pecans.

Chapter 9

"**L**ook, it's Sara," Kaydence, the young Caddo said as the two rode into their territory. The young native sprinted towards the horse.

"Where's John at?" Sara asked, her first words not a cordial greeting.

Kaydence looked a little upset and wondering about the identity of the blonde girl on the back, who never received an introduction. "He's across the way." She pointed down the main path. "I'll take you to him."

Kaydence paced down the mud road, Sara and Rose following behind. Kaydence pointed into a hut, while waiting for Sara to calm a shaking Rose a few yards back.

"I need a favor." Sara rode up to John. "I need you to watch little Rose here for a few days." As they dismounted the horse, Sara told the story. "I plan on taking her out to her uncles up in The Nations. We think her family got murdered down on a small plantation two days' ride from here. I'm being blamed for several of the killings. I need to scout this out, maybe take Kaydence with me. She knows the land better than me. You folks can watch and nurture little Rose here for a few weeks, while we make sure it's okay to get to the border. Then we will return, and I'll take her to the Nations. She says she needs to get to some place called Tulasi, clear up North in the Nations."

"I know Tulasi. It's away from out land, but you are near the Muscogees and should go through Choctaw. They are another civilized tribe." He looked at Sara, reassuringly. They had to arrive in the Nations for peace. They walked out of the hut, his arm around Sara.

Kaydence had overheard the conversation. "I wanna go." She ran to Sara, glancing at her adopted father. Her brown eyes enlarged. A smile emerged on her face. John had a hard time rejecting his adopted daughter's wishes.

"Okay, I suggest you take a different route. Let Kaydence lead the way. She's been out riding looking for you. She's even seen your picture plastered on some shop windows in town."

Sara huffed. In between breaths, she blurted, "They were trying to kill me since they thought I'm this killer. I had to shoot a few people. There was a bounty hunter, and couple ferry operators who tried to rape me too. I got em both. Then the Sabine sheriff and another fool bounty hunter. They both be dead."

John looked at her, acknowledging the rumors. "That's not what the marshal's office told us, but I believe you. They want to rid this state of us, any Negroes or half-breeds, in the area. Any excuse. Right now, they don't have a reason to kick us off the land. We are staying free, minding our business, and we want to keep it that way."

"I can hide here for a few days?"

"Of course. Stay here, we will rest. We will do your hair, give you traditional dress while you're out. In addition, we will teach this youngster to ride like a Caddo."

They replaced the earring in Sara's pierced ears and dressed her in a red wrap. The braids in her hair lowered, starting at her shoulders instead of the top. The woman looked native, though darker than most. Rose measured up for her traditional dress and received the same treatment. She screamed as the local women twisted her hair tight but toughened as the contortion continued. Her ears needed piercing as well.

She screamed as the needle went through her earlobe, her whimper making the women chuckle. Soon they donned her in a turquoise long wrap around dress. Days passed uneventfully. Certain that Rose would be safe here, Sara felt the need to venture out. She hugged the tribe goodbye. A tear descended the moment her eyes rested on Rose. She didn't want to leave the girl alone. Danger existed outside the village; a danger she forbade Rose to see. Kaydence rode up beside Sara, ready to head out. Quietly, like a ghost, John stood before them, tall, his hand held high, stopping the two young women.

"Of course, stay shouting distance behind Kaydence. Get yourself a pistol. I might have one. Use it to signal Kaydence, and for close distances. Logansport is the best place to cross. There should be a ferry there." John beckoned the three girls to the ground. With a stick, he sketched out a map, displaying where they needed to go. "People use that ferry a lot. Keep under cover. You might have to wait a few days."

"They think I headed West, but they spotted us leaving that farm home. I think it's them killers who live there. Once I get this little girl home, I will check it out. I'm trying to put some time between my ferry killings and her family's." "This is a good plan. You did good, Sara. I'm teaching Kaydence how to scout for trouble. She has a good eye and nose for crisis. She spots Coyote for many miles. Same reason I want her to go along, and for you to follow. She will have a weapon if needed. I've taught her how to shoot. Caddi Ayo, The Great Chief in the sky, mentioned you would return and need our assistance."

"Sir, while we were on our way, a great storm hit. I prayed to my protector, and Rose prayed to hers. Will the three different gods keep us safe? They protected us so far."

John rose and looked at the sky, where the sun was setting on the western horizon. He turned East. "I have rejected this little girl's religion; however, I must pretend to believe to stay on the land. We must attend the services yet can't practice ours in public. The white man says that the person you follow is the devil, but they say the same about Caddi Ayo. The white man thinks any God different from theirs is an idol, and its worship a sin. Answering your question, yes, I believe the three gods can and will work together. You speak nice to them, grant them favors, shower them with the gifts, and pray to them. I'm sure you will have your protection."

"I need to make some alcohol. I think that's one of my God's preferred gifts. My mother bought him some, and he does like the best. I want to make some whiskey and have it ready for the trip. I'm not sure where to find him, but I remember he would appear when you presented him with the gift."

John paced around their small renegade commune. He pondered the idea, kicking up mud from the recent storm that softened the earth. He desired this place to be alcohol free. There was a sense of community on this little plot of land the Caddo refuges called home that he wanted to remain that way. One mistake could send them up to the Nations, and have their homeland destroyed.

He noticed the look in the Rose's eyes. A look of an orphan who needed to get with her extended family. Kaydence and Sara needed all the divine intervention possible. He called Joseph, the boy, to scout for a spot, discreet from any marshals or deputies who may check on them.

"Sara, do you know how to make this whiskey?" He locked gaze with her.

She frowned. "I'm not sure, but I know who to ask. It could be the same person who led me here. The same person this gift is meant for. He is my protector, and he has shown me how to make it to his liking. I will talk to him tonight. I will speak with Caddi Ayo as well, if I may, since he is the God of these lands and watches out for my family here."

"I will speak with Caddi Ayo. You mean well, Sara. You are seeking protection for that little girl sitting over there and enjoying a nice dinner of maze and fish. We will tend to her, make her clothes, get you supplies, especially now you can't show your face to any shopkeepers."

After Sara devoured her dinner of fish and maze, she slept in the grass hut alongside her friend Kaydence and Rose. Kaydence dozed off, her breaths heavy. Sara lit her corncob pipe, strolled to the entrance of the small home, and sat on the ground with her legs crossed. A powerful fruity aroma filled the moonlit sky as Sara sent a message to her protector. Done smoking the entire bowl, she repacked her pipe, took another puff and blew three smoke-rings into the night sky. She whispered to the man aiding her from the tornado, the same man who aided her to the Caddo.

"Oh protector, watching out for me. I ask you to protect me, while I take the little girl to the Nations. She is an orphan as her kinfolk disappeared, and there is the rumor of travelers vanishing, and her clan was one of them. I want to shower you with whiskey; however, I lack knowledge on how to make it the way you want it. At the moment, I cannot purchase it. If you have been watching me, I'm sure you understand why. Can you come visit me? You know where I am staying. I will speak with the Great One, Caddi Ayo, as well. We must work together as one. I will make your whiskey, if you show me how. The whiskey will be yours and mine for our journey. Please, sir, I am praying to you for protection." She set a tin of Perique and a spare pipe out by the front entrance. In addition, some dried kernels of maze sat as a gift. With what whiskey she had left, Sara poured half of it into a small jar and set it beside the other presents.

She returned to her bed, tossing and turning in her struggle to fall into deep slumber. A man's husky voice spoke in the night. "I will come visit. You may not recognize me, since I must come protected. I want to protect these people too. They have been good to you. I see your gifts already. When you wake, they will be gone, but look where the Little Elves hide out. They will let me be. Caddi Ayo already has given me his blessing."

Sara snuck out of the hut and waited for the myth to arrive and stared at the gifts beside her, wishing she would see him receive them. She pulled her hat over her eyes and drifted off to sleep again, and then woke with the sun rising in the eastern sky. Gone were the presents and no sign of the man, no callings from the Little Elves. She didn't hear the trees howling, even though the rest of the renegade tribe mentioned it over their first meal of the day.

The breakfast comprised fruits, root vegetables, some deer that were hunted and made into a sausage with eggs from the little farm they ran. Rose ate more than she should, having had nothing but rabbit meat and blackberries for two straight days. She wanted a stack of flapjacks, her last meal with her parents and siblings, but ended up eating until her skinny belly was full.

Sara feasted, enjoying having a meal prepared by the Caddo women. She wanted to help the ladies cook, but they turned down her offer. She was a guest and would leave when John said it was time to go. John always had the best communication with Caddi Ayo. He knew when the time was right. First, the drifter would need his gift. He was scheduled to arrive today, and he and Sara would start work.

A stranger rode up in a small wagon as the Little Elves howled. The man, darker than a white man, but lighter than a Negro, rode up. The race of the man was uncertain. He appeared similar complexion to the girl who would work with him brewing the whiskey. The girl who would present him with his gifts.

One horse pulled the wagon he guided on the small bench. The Elves howled at his presence, soft winds blowing through their commune, while the Caddo turned to watch him drive the buggy.

The old man dismounted slowly. He grasped the brake lever to propel himself to step off. He supported his weight on the rein hitch while stepping down, resting his feet on the clevis until the devil could reach the ground. When he descended, he grabbed his cane, and hobbled over towards Sara and the Shaman. He looked straight at John, shaking his hand. The grip firm but cordial. "I appreciate you letting me come here. I understand this is against your policy, but I am glad you understand the situation. This woman did not ask to be here. It was I who brought her here. There is a reason, and Caddi Ayo and I both fight the coyote as well as the white man. Sara here had been caught in the middle. We will make enough of the whiskey for triple my payment. We do not know how long she will be on her journey. Once the three gallons are gone, I will gather all the supplies and ingredients for the whiskey and vanish. You haven't seen me, so Caddi Ayo will not be aware, and we can't see your Great Spirit, but we all understand he is there."

Sara glanced at the two conversing. This was a meeting for both men. The one mortal, the one immortal. She watched them exchange pleasantries eye; contact direct as they spoke. Patiently, she waited for them to acknowledge her. John turned to her. "Sara," he called out.

She raced towards the men, leaving tracks in the mud, eager to start brewing the whiskey though details needed completed before cooking began. The sun had become a full bright ball on the eastern horizon, the day still in infancy.

The man climbed back into the buggy. Sara followed and sat adjacent to him, allowing him to take the reins. He finagled both horse and buggy through the Pecan trees, and towards the river.

On the alert for a perfect breeding ground to ferment the illegal sauce, he found one sitting behind a bluff alongside the river, and yanked the reins, stopping the pony. "We will build it here. I will tell you how, but only once. We have the required supplies."

The sun screened by pecan trees; the duo operated in the dark. Sara Barnum, a natural craftsperson, put the pieces together. The copper tubes in place, the harnesses all attached, Sara set the large pot over the fire, which had burnt to embering coals. The boiled water had cooled down enough after taking it off the heat.

"Sara, it's okay to pour the maize in the water." He instructed kindly. "Dump slow, stir as you pour it in."

Sara retrieved a couple of sticks, one to pull the maize from the pot, the other she used to stir up mash. In about twenty minutes, the mixture thickened. "Sir, is this good now?"

Taking his time to limp over, the man observed. "That looks good. Simmer these up in the little pan. It sweetens this stuff up." He handed her about a hand basket of cherries. "Take these and sear them up a little."
Sara dumped the berries into a small pan. She cooked the cherries up, stirred them as she went, and added the fruit to the mixture. She blended the ingredients together. The mixture started out thick, but soon liquified.

"Add some of this." He handed her a bag of yeast the Caddo used for making their wonderful bread.

"Did you steal this?" Sara asked.

"Nope, I bought it from the feed store on the way into town, over round Natchitoches. I'm sure they knew what's up." His smile gleamed in the forest.

Sara responded to his grin with one of her own. Her eyes grew bigger, her face turned a little red. She had invited him into her world with the grin. She continued stirring the fruit. She needed the nectar from the fruit, and once it heated enough, she splashed it in.

The cherries added extra flavor, and the fermenting sugar would add an extra kick to the brewing mash.

"Okay, we are done. Let's get a bite to eat."

Meal done; the man drove the carriage back to the commune. He dropped Sara off, and then ventured down the road. The man gone, Sara scarfed down a lunch of cornbread, deer steaks, and blackberries, beside her two friends. It was time Kaydence and Sara learnt to ride as one, time to get their signals straight. It was time to watch her ride, to learn Kaydence's repertoire.

Kaydence needed to scout. She'd need to be aware of every sound and movement ahead of her. The volume of a twig snapping may mean trouble. Kaydence sure was more observant, cautious, and possessing keener instincts than the elder girl she rode with.

They spent the afternoon riding, slicing through the bayou, leaving Rose to get fitted for some clothing the native women made for her as she adjusted to the Caddo customs.

On returning, Sara tended to the still for a few hours before returning to the hut. She repeated the process the next week.

The man disappeared after two days. Sara remained brewing and distilling the alcohol on her own. She tasted it occasionally, and she concluded it tasted better than the bottled, factory-made stuff she purchased from the trader weeks earlier.

Chapter 10

The Grumbel family dined that evening in their small plantation home. Dallas Grumbel, a tall man, owned the trading shop in town, and lived with his wife, Carol. Carol, a stout woman, unable to bear children of her own, helped raise her in-law's seven kids. Dallas's brother, Lawrence Grumbel, worked as a farmer. The Grumbels owned a small plantation with a large barn and two small cabins on the edge of the tree line. Lawrence lived with Greta, a German immigrant, a plump blonde lady with a decent shape even after having seven children. She learned the ways of the American South and Louisiana cooking, which she combined with her German. She spoke in broken English. Most people said she was an amiable lady, but she possessed a crazy streak about her. Lawrence often spent time in the barn, seeking seclusion from his wife.

Frank, the oldest child of Lawrence and Greta, hid out in his cabin. The cabin sat on the border of former Caddo territory. Indian Mounds stood in the background, not over fifteen minutes by horseback. The place was reachable only if one knew about it. It sat off the main trail undetected. Frank was often gone, searching for a woman, or seeking a saloon fight along West Louisiana. He rambled towards Mansfield often, where he kept a cabin. It sat near abandoned Caddo huts, near the graveyard. They lost most of the huts in the Battle of Mansfield. After the war, Frank settled in a remaining shanty outside the village.

A lot of places to hide in both cabins as the Mansfield cabin sat deep in the forest. The Yanks might not even discover it when they burnt their way through the South. Frank used the cabin when he did his debauchery north of the homestead. His kin never doubted him. He was a large young man, strong as an ox, but slow-witted. He was not diabolical. Many said he was too stupid, but he followed instructions to the best of his ability. Frank stocked his cabin with food he stole from covered wagons of strangers. He took care of any evidence, except for the essentials- weapons and food.

He sat on the floor of the cabin, debating whether to head into the saloon or get piss-assed drunk in the cabin. The first night outside Mansfield, he got drunk alone. He desired a woman, whether willing or by brute force.
He finished disposing the covered wagon the next day. He buried it in the mounds, not fifty yards from his little hideaway, and changed clothes into his seeking–a-bride-clothes he'd wear to church if he attended and took the horse into town. His tan pants hung a little short on him. The shirt, an off shade of white, clung to him. He wore a bow tie, which hung crooked from his throat, and the suspenders did nothing to hold his tight slacks on. The man had no need for them, except to look stylish. On his head, he wore a flattened hat. Frank wore a handlebar moustache as well. If his clothes fit, he looked stylish. Folks in the saloon he frequented thought he looked awkward in the fabric. But all those meant nothing to him. He longed for a wife.

Frank refused the prostitutes, or the hookers refused to call on him. It was close to nine in the evening, and figured he should head home, try his luck the next day. He was blessed to receive a new wardrobe and would attempt a second saloon in town. This one, the whores who frequented the establishment, were classier. He figured he'd have a better shot at the classier joint.

Instead of a quick drink this night, he nursed his whiskey, taking slow sips rather than downing shots like he quenched a deep thirst. He admired the prostitutes and other women who frequented the establishment, but was too dim-witted to make a move, or the women did not give him a chance. He watched them walk away. The whiskey went down quicker as Frank took the glass, poured it down his throat, and ordered another one. He slammed down the whiskey, followed by another. He looked around the place. The women hung out with either total strangers, rich, but ugly carpetbaggers, or locals.

He took another snort, slammed the glass down on the bar, and did not flinch as it shattered.

"All right, it's time for you to leave," the bartender screamed at him, his high-pitched voice causing the other men to look over at the ruckus. "You've had enough."

Frank staggered to his feet. He grasped the end of the bar to keep his balance. "Are you going to make me?" He looked like a bear towering above other patrons.

The bartender whipped out his pistol, fired it at no one in particular. "Next time I'm aiming. Get out of here!"

The other men at the bar gathered around like vultures.

"Tom, if you need some help, we'll take care of this retard. The three of us can toss this ox out," the largest of the men retorted. This man, shorter and thinner than Frank, possessed a scar that ran across his face. His skin tone, darker than a Caucasian man, appeared half-bred with either Indian or former slave. Rumors stated he fought off a Yank who attempted to slash him with a bayonet. Other rumors were he received the slash from a grey coat, since the man wanted to desert. Either way, he was a man not to be reckoned with.

The other two men he drank with one were burly, with a thick bushy moustache and beard covering his mouth. The youngest, but tallest member of the group, had thin whiskers, and blonde like his hair, which hung long below a worn cowboy hat.

They worked on a ranch outside of Mansfield towards Logansport and came from the other side of the river but worked in Louisiana.

They paid for the women already. However, another thrill awaited the men. It was the thrill of shooting a slow-witted ox of a man. All pistols cocked- aimed at Frank.

He calculated that getting one or two was a possibility. He may be slow, but not stupid. One man with no weapon against at least three with drawn weapons wouldn't be a fair fight. The laughter of all the patrons followed Frank Grumbel as he stormed out the door in the early evening from the Mansfield Saloon. Sad, frustrated, he kicked the saloon doors open and let it slam shut with such violence that the tavern seemed to rattle. He mounted his horse and rode a few miles east before switching directions, delaying his return to the cabin. The next day, he planned on returning to his home near Pleasant Hill.

Chapter 11

It was time for Kaydence and Sara to head to the river. The key was knowing every move the other girl might make. Sara needed to trust Kaydence's eye. Kaydence had to trust Sara's marksmanship in case of an ambush. They took off, horses galloping. Sara's spotted pony grabbed a quick lead, used to the quick pace she rode. Kaydence's faithful, solid brown colt started a little apprehensive, but his competitive flare took over. Both girls packed for a week's journey.

They headed northwest, following the Red River. They rode side by side for the first few miles before Sara decreased her pace. Kaydence evolved into the scout when they headed towards Texas. The girls knew to turn at the spot marked from a tree they had chopped down earlier. They stopped for a break, eating nuts, fruits, and deer jerky.

They picked up on the journey after dousing the fire. Kaydence led well, her horse veering in and out of the forest, galloping, as it solved the slalom of the curved trail. Sara knew it well. She had taken this path before and rode it often when she stayed with the Caddo. This time she rode fully packed with a loaded six shooters, loaded rifles and her trusty shotgun all within reach. Kaydence had her hunting rifle and her knife. Her shooting was not as good as Sara's, and she lacked the killer instinct. She often chickened out when confronting a deer.

They rode fast without spotting a soul. As though the devil was on their heels, they splashed through a creek with its water surging upwards, behind the hooves of the sprinting equine. Hungry and tired, Kaydence squinted, recognizing the surroundings. Mansfield was in sight. Verifying that Sara's face was not plastered over the doors and windows of Mansfield establishments was needed as well. If no wanted posters existed, the scouting expedition should be peaceful for the duration. But if the sketch of her description sat plastered on each saloon entrance, every trading post, boutique, barber shop and livery stable, they'd have to sneak through town.

Kaydence stopped at the clearing beside the last rows of trees upon a small bluff. The town sat a mere fifty yards before her. She gazed through her field glasses, detecting nothing unusual. Drunken men shuttled through saloons. One man who stumbled out a saloon door looked intoxicated but harmless. Spinning her head to look behind, she searched for her riding partner. Sara's horse trotted through the forest. She reduced pace as they approached her friend. Sara took off her hat, swished her hair back, and dismounted. She lifted her arms above her head and attempted to separate her body from her legs in a stretch. Walking around her horse, she questioned her friend. "Anything unusual?" Kaydence dismounted. She patted her horse's head. The animal glanced at her, her finger on her lips to keep it quiet. The horse never whinnied.

Kaydence stepped forward. "Nothing unusual. Just a couple of men walking around. I suppose that happens in a town this size."

"Yeah, going from tavern to tavern, it appears. Think you should check it out, or wait until morning?"

"The sun is setting. Less chance of being seen. I'll check it out. If it's all clear, we can get through town and bunk out."

Sara glanced at the setting sun. The orange ball dropping rapidly into the horizon. A quick spin through town before passing still seemed plausible to the girls.

"Okay, I'll cover you, just in case." Sara pulled the rifle from her saddlebag. Additional bullets rested in her vest. The girl could reload in a hurry, so it's best to be prepared.

Kaydence remounted her pony. They trotted through town, parading the main street, checking out the doors and windows of the establishments. Being Caddo, she was still in enemy territory. Though her people and the history stated they were a peaceful group, however, the townspeople couldn't tell the difference between Caddo and Comanche.

Sara kept her eye on Kaydence, glancing away long enough to check out pedestrians. The oversized drunkard passing to another saloon raised suspicion. Sara replaced the field glasses with her rifle, waiting for Kaydence to ride past the man.

A drunken Frank Grumbel strolled out of the saloon, searching for the horse he rode in on. Oblivious to his surrounding, he staggered past Kaydence, who missed him, while searching terrible sketches of her friend, and not paying attention to events in front of her. Frank Grumbel noticed the slow-moving horse about to collide with him and the attractive young native girl aboard it. "Watch where you going?" He slurred in a drunken stupor.

Kaydence drew her pistol too late.

"You are coming with me." He threw her off the horse, sending her pistol to the dirt. He dragged her forward by her arms. Come back with me. I know you they break you Injuns in early. If not, I be breaking you in rough. He dragged her, making Kaydence stagger to get to her feet.

Sara fired a warning shot from the rifle. She shot close enough to miss, and the dirt flew up a mere ten feet from the man. He swung and rode forward around the corner. Sara, with no view of them, rode quick, but not fast enough to stop the man from lifting the girl and tossed her on his horse. The black pony carried them off west of town, wild shots ringing behind them. Sara stayed in hot pursuit.

Even drunk, the slow-witted fat boy evolved into an expert equestrian weaving towards his hideout. A commotion came from the behind Sara, she herself pursued. It wasn't the best place to be an Indian. Even worse- a Creole.

"That's her, the girl in the drawing," the roughnecks shouted.

"The reward gonna be ours," another one screamed, hot on Sara's tail. Frank headed for the cabin a few miles southwest of town, Kaydence sitting behind him; hands tied around his thick waist. He still finagled the horse through the forest. Sara fell back, unable to make up ground, while the drunk rough necks kept an ample distance behind her.

Frank, intent on getting his jollies with the native girl, arrived at the cabin about ten minutes ahead of Sara, who struggled to tail him. He shoved Kaydence into the cabin, tore her clothes off and panted, with her young body inviting him towards her. He slapped and tossed her on the bed. Not taking his eyes off her, he tore off his shirt, covered her face, taking up too much time with his tortuous attempt at raping the young girl.

Sara kicked the door open and walked into Kaydence's screams. Her voice muffled from the shirt tied around her face. The man, focused on ravaging and raping his conquest, paid little attention to the interruption.

Sara, aware of the men following her, would burst in the door in about fifteen minutes at the earliest, figured one shot would do it. They'd be in and out and lost in the forest again.

She shot the man in the back and watched him fall like a pecan tree during a hurricane. "Get up, we gotta run." Sara slashed the ropes and around Kaydence's arms, and pushed the shirt from Kaydence's face. "Hop on, Papa." She named her steed. Kaydence ran out and mounted the animal. Sara climbed on in front.

West, towards Texas, they did not stick around to explain themselves. Sara once again made her kill, quick, painless, and efficient. She developed a future for herself as an assassin. She tallied six in a month, but she didn't count. All were self-defense, or defending a friend. Papa galloped deep into the forest and stopped short of the next town, Logansport.

Chapter 12

The men entered Frank's hideaway cabin in search of evidence. They discovered one body amongst Frank's interior possessions. Frank's body laid face down, soaked in his blood.

Their anger profound, the men kicked the body. Paul, the youngest of the men, not much older than a boy, looked at the two older cowboys. "I think we should leave this fat boy laying in his blood. He had some young squaw with him. I saw him smack and grab her. He could have tried to rape and kill the girl." The kid, whiskers attempting to cover his face, wore a vest over a flannel shirt, jeans, and a cowboy hat. "We should go to the sheriff. Tell him what we saw." "Nah," the middlemen said. "There's a reward for dat girl. If we catch her, bring her back dead or alive, we split that reward."

The two debated, each attempting to win the other over. The man with the scar across his cheek and dressed in black, paced the floor, smoking a cigar. His glance shuttled between his partners and the body. Disgusted, he flicked ash on the corpse and sent a blob of saliva mixed with tobacco juice on as he spoke.

"We wanted to kill this fat mother fucker. He ruined our night. We were gonna get Paul a girl tonight. Them whores were digging on him. At least that girl took care of it for us. Besides, there is a five-hundred-dollar reward for her. If we report this to da sheriff, the parish sheriff and marshal over here gonna keep da money. These Louisiana lawmen are crooked, not like back in Texas. We might have to let her go. Looks like she was protecting her friend from that oaf. In which case, we need to get the fuck out of here before any law comes and put the blame on us."

The middleman gaped at the leader. "We gonna let her go?"

Paul chimed in. "Look over here, there are some native jewels on da floor, and it looks like he ripped them off her. This fucker was trying to rape that young squaw. I think that little nigger girl was protecting her. You know they look out for one another, since some of them live on the reservations together. I think we should go back. That youngest whore liked me, anyway. I hope they are still there." He headed towards the door, attempting to be the leader.

The scar-faced man stopped him. "Wait, I bet they are heading towards the border. We can get to Logansport tonight, hijack the ferry and catch them. Those two girls don't know what we look like, but we'll recognize them. Plus, we can always use a good shooter. I think we could have them ride with us."

A smile appeared on the kid's youthful face. "I'd like that. I like the way she rode, plus this is a purdy picture of her." He tore off a wanted picture of Sara, which was plastered on saloon wall earlier.

"You want a woman? That's why we came into town." The middleman looked at Paul. "I still think we should nab da girls. Let's get that little nigger and the young squaw. Hell, I bet we could trade dem off. Probably virgins, so we could get some good money."

"Nah, we don't trade them for money. We keep em. Use them to rob the trains, have them distract the engineer, have them go into banks. Them girls have way more value than a reward, or a payoff from Comanches." The scar faced man put out his cigar on the dead fat man. He twisted it into the man's arms, filling the space with the wrench scent of burning flesh. The outlaws left the cabin, mounted their horses, and returned to town. They expected the whores waiting for them. It did not disappoint them upon arrival.

Chapter 13

Sara and Kaydence slipped back into town. They grabbed Kaydence's horse and snuck back into the forest west of town. Getting Rose to her uncle's was still a priority. Little did they know the outlaws rode past them into town, seeking the gratification they desired.

Kaydence slept while Sara stood guard, all her weapons loaded, her knife sat out of the sheath, while she paced around her friend asleep by the campfire. Sara wanted to talk to her about the attack, but put it aside for later. They had time. The night was quiet when they switched places.

Up before sunrise, the girls extinguished the fire and rode off. The goal was still the river, though more caution was required. They debated riding adjacent to one another.

"Do you want to talk about it?" Sara asked Kaydence as they trotted through the trees into a clearing.

"Not yet, maybe when we slow down again." Kaydence kicked her horse. The steed whinnied, took off and raced its way across the field. Sara soon was on her tail. They trotted adjacent once again.

"I was scared, since I thought that man was going to kill or rape me. I'm so glad you came along when you did. No man or boy has ever touched me like that before. The elders keep a watchful eye out for me."

"I never done nothing with a boy either, since I am kind of scared to do things. I had me a vision. That's why I want to talk to you about it. I think he wants me to protect us Indians and freed girls from these guys, who wants us for their pleasure." Sara smiled. "I guess that's why I got these." She raised her rifle, pointing it towards a clearing. "Stop here, Kaydence. I think I see a deer."

"Wait, Sara, don't shoot. I hear something."

Sara kept the gun aimed. "Where at?" she whispered.

"Behind us. I heard branches cracking. Might be coyote coming after us, might be the law, or someone chasing us. Think we should split and meet at the next town? I can head through this trail. It looks like it splits in two towards the clearing, and Logansport should be right past the tree line."

Sara pondered over the idea. "Where shall we meet up later? I like your idea of splitting up. You head that way, while I go this way." She pointed towards the southwest skies. "I'll let you ride ahead for a couple of minutes."

They rode off as planned. When they got to the tree line at the east end of town, Kaydence waited for Sara. Again, both girls ventured past the saloons and trading posts. Logansport, busier than Mansfield because of its geography, sat adjacent to the Sabine, with a view of Texas on the other side of the river. It was a rougher place than Mansfield because of the trappers who did business at the trading posts.

The girls rode the streets seeking posters of Sara, the cold-blooded killer, but could not find any.

"Let's bunk here in town. We can get us a room, or I bet we can flop somewhere inside. Some of the local whores might know a place where we can bed down. Hoping we don't have to work for a room."

Kaydence scowled. "What do you mean? Clean floors, bring them food or something?"

Sara fell off the horse from laughing so hard. "Oh, Kaydence, you're so naïve. Don't ya know what they do in da whorehouses? Them boys go in and drop fifty cents to da girls so they can screw em. It's a living, but not a good one. Nuttin I plan on doing, but I'm sure none of da whores planned on doing that either." She mounted the horse again. "Let's go check da river out. Make sure it's safe crossing. Then I think it's best to skedaddle."

Kaydence followed behind her this time as they rode towards the river. On the bank sat a couple of boats. The girls saw several men unloading cotton from one boat and putting the bales on a freight train to head in some direction. Sara was more concerned about being noticed, despite the absence of rough sketches or an artist's renderings of her facial features.

She thought neighboring towns would share information, but the place looked safe. All she had to do was to return with Rose to the makeshift commune they settled in, cross at the ferry, and be free to roam the swamps of East Texas, even venture north to the Red River and cross into the Nations. It was sure bound not to be easy, especially with a close call not less than twenty-four hours prior.

They led their horses to the river for a drink of water. One of the younger riverboat workers came up to Kaydence. He was tall, over six feet, but had a youthful look on his baby-face with no whiskers. His eyes, soft, without a hint of trouble, looked straight at her. He grinned and, with his long arms, waved a group of ten men over. The men, grittier than the boy, strolled over at a pace the tortoises and snails matched. Sara's and Kaydence's breath became heavier while their heartbeat accelerated. Sara studied their movements. The men formed a semi-circle as if they rehearsed their placements the last time young females dropped by unattached. She looked over at her friend. Her horse's snout remained in the river, lapping up the flowing water.

Kaydence waited for her steed to quench his thirst. She peered at her friend and glanced back at the men. The circle widened, setting a trap for them as the males separated. It was time to leave. Kaydence lifted the reins, pulled her horse away from the water, and turned it around. She took off, straight through the center of the men, with Sara trailing behind her. The horses kicked as they fled the river's edge, rode through town, and exited the forest. Behind them, the sun started its descent. They needed to bunk down, and after their horses received their refreshment, they would begin some night riding. The girls took advantage of the remainder of the daylight, riding hard, cutting through the trees, vanishing from the larger city with no one on their trail. Positive they were not being followed; Sara reduced the pace along the northern trail Kaydence took earlier.

After spending the night with their ladies of the evening and having a big breakfast, the three outlaws galloped towards town. At a split in the trails, west of Mansfield and near Logansport, they sat and debated which trail to take. They chose the southern route, bypassing the girls about halfway, all parties oblivious to one another. The girls set up camp for a few hours.

As soon as they entered town at sunset, the men began their search for women of the night. They found them in a nice saloon and delved into another evening of drunken debauchery, intending to implement their plan the next day. After breakfast and a soothing bath, the men rode towards the ferryboat on the Texas side. The scar-faced man lifted his pistol and waved it across the river.

"You seen two girls pass this way? One a little younger than me, the other a tad bit younger. The younger might have been an Injun, the other one, I got no idea what she was, maybe a quadroon."

The tall boy looked at the outlaw kid with a grin. "Yeah, there were a couple of girls here. Took off out of town. I'm not sure where they went. Headed back towards downtown, but that was the last I saw of them. I was hoping they might spend the night. Would have liked to shack up with them."

"You know one's wanted, don't ya? Killed some guy over in Mansfield, but the jerk deserved it, plus she's wanted for some other killings down south. You might be lucky they left."

"Hell, there are a bunch of us. We can handle it."

The gangly kid's group commenced the same formation; however, the outlaws were not playing. A few of the men standing at the outside of the semi-circle clenched their pistols. They did not know what hit them. The hothead, the quickest draw in the East Texas, took out the first six he shot. They dropped on the spot. The kid stabbed the taller youth he was speaking with in the chest and fired at the remaining four. The deaths were sudden, except for the tall youth, who squirmed in a pool of his own blood panting, before the scar-faced man gave him a fatal shot that put him out of his misery.

The ferry operators, the Hardy brothers, witnessed the massacre, but they had already pulled the boat ashore. The men making mental notes of the killers never saw their demise, since the man with the scar slashed across his face boarded the watercraft, and his gang accompanied him.

"You do as I say." A pistol pointed at the older Hardy brother. He dressed well as the ferrying business was successful, while his brother, who did the major labor tugging the craft across the river, dressed more casual, overalls and a straw hat. Two pistols pointed at him.

"Why did you kill them?" the older brother asked.

The man with the scar across his face smiled and lit a cigar. The stogie fired up even in the breeze. He took a few puffs to keep it burning. "We don't want any witnesses." He cocked his pistol at the older ferry operator. "Walk backwards. I hope you can swim."

The river waters flowed briskly as they approached the channel near the center. Even the best swimmer could never survive the current. The older Hardy brother didn't move, but made no attempt to challenge the outlaw with his pistol. The outlaw pulled the trigger. There was a click. The Hardy brother flinched as this repeated five times before retreating to the edge of the craft. It didn't take much of a shove for the outlaw to nudge the operator into the flowing current.

The other brother had no chance against the other two outlaws. He took a dive. No one witnessed the man surfacing. The outlaws assumed he drowned and tugged the boat to the other side of the river.

The kid looked up at the leader, eyes wide at the Texas sky. "What we gonna do?"

"We wait. In da meantime, we run a little ferrying business, make a few bucks, and if the law comes after us, we can sail on down."

"Right, kid," the crazy man, the quick draw specialist, exclaimed. "We sit here and run this ferry. Act like nothing gonna happen. Just like old scar-face says. We know who is in charge and it ain't me bailing us out of every situation." The man admired his pistol, reloaded the Colt, and aimed it at scar-face. "Bam," he said, returning the pistol back in its holster. "I don't like waiting, though. Might need to find some action here on the other side."

"Nah." The leader took off his hat and wiped the thick black bush of hair with his hand. "We lie low, do some good deeds if need be, wait for them two girls to come back, and feed them with promises."

"What if they don't come back?" the kid asked, still wide-eyed.

"I know they will return." He spat tobacco juice into the river. "I know they are coming. I got me inside information. Devil told me last night."

Paul chewed on his loose-leaf tobacco, spat the entire wad out. He turned his head and smirked.

Chapter 14

The ride back to Kaydence's home went without a glitch. They rode at night, slipping through Mansfield when the night sky was pitch black. No one wandered the streets. From there, it was another two days' home. They rode hard, rested when they could, and arrived at the commune as the sun rose. The elves greeted them with howls. James and the rest of the clan came out to meet them. When little Rose emerged, Sara and Kaydence struggled to recognize her with hair that used to be in pigtails, now in braids, and fell to her side. She dressed in traditional Caddo; a red dress wrapped in a deer-skin shawl. Her face creased into a smile as she ran to hug Sara, her new mother.

Kaydence dismounted from her horse and went over to the Shaman, her surrogate father. "We had problems in this town."

"Mansfield," Sara explained. "I got recognized, and they tried to rape Kaydence. Some guy grabbed her, and I went chasing after them. Then some other guys came chasing after me. We eluded them, but I'm not sure about heading that way."

"I'm glad Sara was with me, since that fat man scared me so. We got to this cabin where he pulled his pants down. That's when Sara shot him. She saved my life."

The Shaman studied the girls. His gaze remained on the orphan girl. "Did you speak to Caddi Ayo before you departed, Kaydence?"

Kaydence looked away from her father in shame. "No," she muttered inaudibly.

"Always speak to Caddi Ayo. The Great Spirit is there to protect you. He will keep you safe."

Rose watched the interaction between the native girl and her surrogate. She suddenly felt alone, missing her father.

"Is the Caddi-yo like Jesus? I was praying to Jesus to protect you. I prayed every night, and you came back to take me across Texas. He didn't protect my family since they killed them, but he protected me. My pa always said there is a plan, and sometimes we don't know what it is."

"Rose, yes, Caddie Ayo is like Jesus, but they are so different. I will not say which God is better. I talk to Caddie Ayo, and he has kept us safe here, even though the white man wants us to talk to Jesus, his God." He grabbed Rose's hand, urging her towards the end of the commune. He pointed in the direction where the whiskey sat brewing. "See that man over there?"

Rose squinted, unable to make out the man, though she felt his presence. "I…I…think so. Same man who shows up when you believe in him. That is what Sara told me, when we rode up here."

"Yes, and he's not always to be trusted. Sara and him made a deal. He will be protecting both you, Kaydence, and Sara on your journey. He may look like an old man, but if you love him, like you love the White Man Jesus and respect Caddi Ayo, he will protect you. You girls will have three Gods watching over you on your journey. One thing you must remember is to love each God equally. Not one God reigns over another. They are not false idols. They may be different; however, their mission remains the same; to protect you."

Sara joined them. "Can I talk to your God over there?" Sara did not understand the man she worshipped for protection and showered with gifts. He preferred the perique tobacco and the whiskey, not approved gifts within the white man's church, or the Caddo. Sara, unsure of the communication ritual, glanced at the Native, the man able to communicate with Great Spirits.

"No, you must communicate with your own God, not this man. I am blessed, since I can speak with all three. Maybe one day, when you learn that man's tricks, you can communicate with him. Right now, you must stay with me, or keep away from him. I won't even let Kaydence speak with him. Only Sara and myself are allowed conversation." He glanced over at the man. Whispering would not keep the man from hearing them.

Sara returned to the house to speak with John in private. They walked to the furthest corner of the grass hat. "He's already playing tricks; I can feel it. If I follow along, we will be safe. It may leave a mark on Kaydence's name, but I will take care of her, while Jesus will protect Rose. Not sure what we will have to do, but it won't be pretty. Kaydence will return to you alive and in one piece. We shall leave after two more sunsets." Sara stood up, shook out her brown hair, and walked out to find the girls.

They saw her first, but she raised a finger, signaling them to wait for her, and strolled towards them.

The man gave the brew a quick taste. He removed his straw hat, not minding that it falls to the ground. Dust blew like a mini tornado the moment he sampled the brew. He stared at the young woman heading his way. She sat beside him on a fallen log and waited. He slid the canning jar with the splash of whiskey under his nose, inhaling the rough aroma of the special whiskey he preferred. His grin meant she did good. He sipped the liquid, leaned back and closed his eyes tight as the liquor streamed down his throat.

"Whoop!" the trickster screamed. "You made it the way I like. I'll make sure you will always make my whiskey." He bowed as if he prayed, though it might have been to give Ms. Barnum a blessing. Sara heard him mumble, "give her the power to make this for me at all times whenever I need my whiskey." The rest of his words rolled on unintelligibly.

"I did good then?" She smiled.

He smarted his lips. "It's the best. I added some magic to it, it's our special magic. Surprisingly, I didn't have to add too much. You have a knack for making this. I am making sure you return safe from your journey. I'll need an eternal supply." He winked, disappearing into the bayou. His head peeked from a moss-covered cypress tree for a final comment before vanishing like the vaporized mash. "It needs another twenty-four hours of aging. I know my whiskey, and you must take a jug with you. I guarantee you will need it."

She headed for the still to study how the man assembled the brewing machine. Now she had the power to make it, and nothing else mattered. Sara brushed her hands together and walked towards the camp. A little distance away, Kaydence and Rose played, the young girl chasing the Indian girl in a futile attempt to catch her. Kaydence let the kid her close in, and then took off sprinting like a deer. Rose threw up her hands in defeat.

"Sara," Kaydence acknowledged her friend. Rose caught up as they both bent at the waists searching for breath. "John says we must go to the mounds, sit by the eternal fire, and speak with Caddi Ayo."

The two girls headed across the clearing, towards the mounds they used as a temple. Rose raced after them, her braids flopping in the breeze. Kaydence turned around. "You can't follow us. This is where we pray. Right now, we must pray separate. You must pray to your Jesus and ask for our protection. The Shaman has told me this, and the Great Spirit will work for us."

Rose stopped dead in her tracks. She watched the girls disappear into the great mound.

Sara and Kaydence sat over the fire that seemed to burn forever. The logs set up in a cross so that the fire glowed in the center. The girls sat across from one another, each with their legs crossed. Sara spoke, but Kaydence put her finger to her lips, hushing her friend. "I must pray first in silence. Once I am done, you must pray in quiet as well. We must pray for the same thing, and you will realize what to pray for from my silent prayer."

Sara had no clue how she would know if they prayed for the exact thing, if the prayer was silent. She wasn't one to question spirits. After all, she followed the trickster. They would be safe.

They bowed in silence, eyes on the flame burning from the center of the cross. The flames of the eternal fire cast shadows across their faces. Neither of the girls smiled as they raised their heads. Kaydence's thick lips curled out as Sara rose. She squinted at the feeling that something was not right with Sara's actions. Sara dealt with her own God, a trickster, who might bring sin into their path. Caddi Ayo told had her to be careful of the man's tricks. He was likely to lure them along a path they did not want to go.

The two girls left the hut together in search of Rose, who sat in their little grass hut they called home.

She spoke out loud, "Lord Jesus, please help me find my uncle in Injun country, and protect my friends Sara and Kaydence. We're on a trip and need your help. I'm not sure they believe in you since they prayed to another God. Also, if my family is in heaven, watch out for them and if they are still alive, I want to see them. Amen."

Sara and Kaydence walked past the hut to talk. "Poor girl, she's an orphan, and the lone reason she's alive is she went for a walk. The man who tried to rape you handled the death of her kin and didn't act alone. There are people still out there."

"Her hope is eternal, like the flame. Father says I should not bring her towards Caddi Ayo yet. You are not to lead her to the one he calls the trickster. Father is aware of the one called The Trickster, and only you can deal with him. We cannot speak with the God white man call Jesus, since he only suits for Rose. She believes he will give her eternal life, and that she will reunite with her family after she joins them. She needs hope, and white man's Jesus, Caddi Ayo and The Trickster will protect us."

Sara stared at Kaydence, battling with herself as if to say something. "Can I tell you my vision when we spoke with Caddi Ayo? I need to see if this is accurate."

"I would speak with my John if you questioned the vision."

"Okay, I must go speak with him. You watch Rose." She raced over to speak with The Shaman. John sat by an open fire cooking up some meat one of his brothers had shot. "Sara, how can I help you?" His eyes found Sara. He knew she meant business.

"Oh John, when Kaydence and I were speaking to Caddi Ayo, I saw. Kaydence told me to talk to you. I have told no one, but I need to seek the trading post tonight. Something will happen. Something to do with the people I have shot and left for dead. Would the Great Spirit tell me to go?" Or is my God, the one you call the Trickster, playing a trick on me, or Caddi Ayo?"

He turned his head toward the embering flames, head bowed. Unintelligible words grunted from him, resembling speaking in tongues. "Sara, come sit," he commanded.

Sara took her time to wander over across the flame from him. The wind blew the smoke towards her, but she did not wave it away. She felt the presence that the smoke swirled towards her.

"You have killed six people, because someone else has been murdering families traveling across here. I have seen the wagons and heard the rumors when I go into town. You must confront them. You must seek the truth. Go tonight, but return for your journey."

"If I don't make it back?"

"You will. There is assistance out there. We will gather our belongings in readiness to ride out after two sunrises. Ride off." It was a command, like she was in the military. She mounted Papa.

"Go before Kaydence wants to tag along. I will let her know."

She sat on top of her horse, armed with a rifle, shotgun, and pistol. The knife lay in her sheath. She pranced off on Papa's back, leaving the compound. The little elves howled at her, their voices carrying, even as the wind picked up. Kaydence, hearing the hooves clopping along the mud and hearing the chiming elves, ran out of the hut.

"Sara, wait," she called, but it was too late.

Her surrogate father rushed towards her. "This is somewhere she must go. There is unfinished business that needs taken care of. Something happened before she returned to us. She must clear her name with The Trickster, Caddi Ayo, and the White Man's God before you make your journey."

Chapter 15

Greta Grumbel and her sister-in-law prepared breakfast. Flour scattered on a lot of visible surfaces in the kitchen as Greta stirred the gravy. She added black and red pepper into the mixture. Carol placed the uncooked biscuits into the wood-burning stove, while Dallas and Lawrence discussed business and farming.

Both men drew on their cigars, filling the dining area of Dallas's home with smoke. "Frank's not home yet?" He questioned his brother, taking another puff of the cigar.

"Nope, the wagon's gone by the time I rode by. His horse is still there, but there was no sign of him." He glanced at the newspaper Dallas set down. Lawrence could not read or write, but enjoyed the etchings on the paper. "He sometimes stays up there in Mansfield."

"Yeah, but for a day or two. It's been a week. The retard should be home by now. Don't ya think you should head up there and look for him?"

"I'm sure he'll be back today." Lawrence replied without taking his eyes off the paper.

His brother twirled the handles of his moustache, occasionally glancing at the ladies in the kitchen. Dallas stuffed his half-smoked cigar into the large ashtray on the dining room table. "You didn't hear me, did you? I said you should head up to Mansfield today."

"I didn't ask you. Leave after breakfast. I could not care about Frank. He was stupid, a retard, might be better off dead, anyway." He lowered his voice, so the women didn't hear. "I care about us getting caught. That half-breed girl riding around has that missing girl, you know."

"I'm sure they are headed towards Texas."

"You said that the last time. You were careless this time." He snapped his trap as the ladies walked in with a pan of gravy and a platter of biscuits. The aroma of the Louisiana breakfast engulfed the anger coming from the Grumbel's dining area. The Grumbels ate in silence after saying grace, thanking Jesus for all their blessings in life, plus they prayed for their brother.

After the family finished with the morning meal, Lawrence excused himself to whisper something to Greta. She looked mad about what he was saying to her, but there was nothing she could do about it. Her husband got up and left out the back door. Dallas strapped up the wagon and rode to the trading post to begin an honest day's work. Greta and Carol remained at the house working on the garden, hiding any evidence that might have been scattered around.

The three outlaws rode their fresh-claimed ferry down the Sabine River. They landed their new raft on the Louisiana side beside another ferry. Two decaying bodies still laid there, chomped by different swamp creatures, but still intact.

The kid poked the two ripped corpses with a downed cypress branch. He glanced towards the leader. "Don't think we should bury dem or something? I mean, they have been lying dead here for a while. Looks like a few weeks now, but no one never said no rights for them, I bet. All people should have rights said for them at death."

He poked the bodies one more time. The scar-faced leader ripped the log away from the kid, tossed it in the river, and made a face at the maggots scurrying away from the body. It seemed the scar-faced man disgusted even the larva of insects. He grabbed another log lying around and poked one of the human carcasses in what remained of his stomach. He whirled the stick around above his head for a complete rotation.

"I'll give him a proper burial," he said tossing the human remains and the log into the Sabine. "Them mighty catfish will get themselves a treat, and some fool will catch it and clean it up. That's da only way someone will find da body."

He repeated the act with the other body. It was in worse shape than the first. The splash sounded like a child tossed a boulder into the river. All three outlaws mounted their horses once they finished tying the ferry up. They trotted up the trail towards town with the scar-faced leader leading the way, followed by the sharp-shooter. The kid trailed them by about fifteen yards.

"If I remember right, there's an old-fashioned trading post not too far from here. We need to get some grub. Plus, we need to get rid of some evidence from up north. Figure we can trade it in for some jerky and tobacco." He sped up, sending the horse galloping down the trail. "Woah." He pulled the black stallion to a halt. "Damn, if ain't another dead body. This guy looked like a mess in his time. Bet he's a bounty hunter."

"Bounty hunters got families, too. I knew this kid when I was in the orphanage, whose pa was a bounty hunter. He went searching for a couple confederates passing this way, and never heard from him again. That man, though, looks nuttin' like him. Still, he might have family."

"You are going soft, kid?" The sharpshooter pulled a pistol on his young partner. The revolver barrel brushed against the kid's ear and then yanked away. "We don't need more than three people in this gang anyway, and we recruiting da girl. You go soft, we don't need ya." He tried to smile but was incapable of displaying a grin.

The sharpshooter glared at the leader. "You gonna bring Mathilda back instead of that new girl? I miss Mattie riding with us. She was always good on those lonely nights, when you got yourself too drunk." His moustache covered the up curled lip in a sinister smile.

The leader looked at the pistolero. One glare told it all. If there was a person being replaced, it would not be the kid. The scar faced man didn't even have to pull a pistol out. One glance was all it took for the gunslinger to replace the pistol in the holster.

"Kid, help ol' Billy get that dead bounty hunter on his horse. He gonna ride off and dispose of da body. It's way too close to da trail." The leader said.

They pried Sara's first kill off the ground with a couple of sticks and placed the body on the horse. Billy mounted in front of the corpse, taking care not to breathe in the aroma of dead human decomposed flesh. "This man stinks to high heaven. I ain't taking him too far off the path." He kicked the horse, both man and animal, galloping towards the bayou.

"That motherfucker gonna get us killed before our time. Do you want the honors?" He handed the kid his pistols, both loaded with six bullets each. "Take care of him. Now!"

The kid swallowed hard, spun, at the same time pulling the triggers on both guns. He shot his former partner in the back while still atop the galloping horse. They never saw him fall. After a good hour's wait, the equine didn't show up.

The kid breathed uneasily. "I think we're both destined for hell, sir. This cold-blooded killing can't be good." He walked towards his horse, ready to move on.

"You know what, I don't believe in no heaven, I don't believe in no hell. Only people who judge us are the town folks. Along the way, if we can get rid of the scum, we looked like heroes. Those boys on da river, they were scum buckets. Do you wanna know why they scum buckets?" He mounted his black stallion, ready to lead to town. "Ask me why, kid?"

The kid pondered the reason. The fear of giving his boss an incorrect answer got the best of him. Better to ask than give an incorrect answer. "Sir, I don't know,but they seemed like hard working folks, just trying to make a buck like everyone else."

Tobacco was spat on the muddy ground by the leader, and the brown spit hid in with the mud. "The boys, sons of the federacy, they want to keep all of us mixed and freedmen down. Didn't think you know about me? I can tell you got some Injun blood in you, too. That's why you are still living and breathing. Me, grandma born a slave over in Mississippi, sold to a plantation by Coushatta. I ran off before the war and have been on the lam ever since getting rid of da grey coats. Them carpetbaggers are just as bad."

"Well, we can't be killing all of them, can we?"

"If we have to, we will. And that girl you saw her, her grandma, be a born slave too. I know she is coming to the store. I got me a vision. She working with da devil."

"I thought you don't believe in no heaven and hell."

"I don't, but I know of this man. He exists, and we work for him. Now let's head out of here."

The kid had one more question, but he savored his life more than obtaining answers. He had heard rumors about a woman named Mathilda, a scorned lover of the leader and the kid's partner, Jack LeRoux, whose mystic powers were often debated between the outlaws.

Both men rode through the swamps, creating their own little trails that they hoped would be undetected by any locals. They rode by some former slave cabins, most of which were abandoned, with about two of which looked occupied. Curtains draped the cut-out windows, horses stayed hitched up to wooden posts. Okra, corn, along with other vegetables and fruits scattered in the field. The man and the kid paid them no mind, continuing their journey.

"There must be a plantation house coming up here aways. Old slave cabins here. Looks like a small plantation we riding on." The kid hollered at his partner.

"Yep, you be learning. I am teaching you well. Stay with me. You do mighty fine."

They came upon a house with a barn that looked taken care of, nothing mysterious about it, but this was Louisiana. Nothing can be taken for granted.

"I smell me some pecan pie cooking," the kid howled over to the man as they neared the house. "Maybe it be cooling off in an open window, and we can get us a treat."

"Nah, we gonna keep on riding. That old trading post up here pretty soon." He looked at the sun, which had set behind them. "Plus, we gonna meet that girl at the post up yonder. She should be there about sunset."

The kid longed to steal a pie, but he had seen what the man with the scar on his face could do. Afraid of his boss, he kept fast on his trail. Soon they hit the trading post with just furs to trade and nothing else. The men walked around the shop. Plastered on the door was a wanted poster of a young woman. The leader ripped it off the door. He leered over the poster and motioned to the kid, who followed him off towards the woods. "This is our girl."

"She's a purdy little one, or I should say that is one good drawing of her." The kid's eyes glinted, impressed with the sketch.

"Hands off of her. This is da girl who be riding with us. We be meeting her tonight. Word is she killed a bunch of people. Probably killed them people we disposed of today, plus we saw her get that guy up north. We need not cross her."

"We should ride up further and meet her and use her to get supplies. We'd scare the crap out of the owner here, and I'm sure we'll get a better price."

"That's why you riding with me, kid. Let's head up, see if we can get her. You hide off in the forest. She's expecting only me."

Chapter 16

Sara Barnum rode Papa hard across the bayou. She had ridden this part of the trail and knew exactly where she was heading. She leaned over her Papa as they galloped across farmland, then cut through the trails meandering through the pecan trees. At the end of the tree line, she spotted an odd one that seemed to thump a tambourine. She brought the horse to an abrupt stop.

"We meet," the tall man with a thick bushy beard, black hat, and a scar slashed across his face said to her. He looked at the picture he had torn off the trading post, narrowed his gaze at the girl and then back at the wanted poster. "Pretty flattering portrait, don't ya think?"

Sara swallowed hard, but unafraid. "Why am I supposed to meet you here?" She knew the answer.

The young male outlaw ogled her, checking her slight frame up and down. He took in the dark straight hair that escaped from beneath her tan hat, not missing her fine brown complexion, tanned by the searing Louisiana sun. Her thin womanly frame filled out in the right places. The young man, who had turned eighteen a few days earlier, succumbed to women's charms. He craved repeat performances.

Sara Barnum paid the young, tall, sandy-haired man no mind. She cared less about his ponytail falling straight from his dark hat. His frame appeared well-sculpted, but she wasn't seeking an assistant. Her vision was to seek out an older man who received a similar glimpse. Both were called to meet at the trading post for a reason, and aware they were under watchful eyes of an outside spirit.

Sara glanced at the portrait of her. For a rough sketch, it was pretty good. It highlighted her assets; the hair falling below the hat, her brown eyes and a youthful face smiling into the future. Her skin tone was correct, darker than a reb, lighter than a slave woman's, and not an injun. "I guess that's me. You're not after a reward, are you?"

"Hell, this is only a thousand dollars." He spat. Her gaze stayed on the tobacco juice on the ground until it absorbed into the mud. When he had her attention, he continued. "I'm sure there's a much bigger reward for me west of the river, over in Texas."

"Why am I supposed to meet you here?"

"I got the same vision. I want you to ride with the boy and I. Saw you shoot that no good fat man down."

Her eyes darted over to the young man, then returned.

"He had my friend, probably was going to rape her, maybe kill her. I had to save her life. Shooting comes natural to me."

"We need a third member, since somewhere along the way, we lost our third member. I suppose this trail of decomposing bodies is your work, too?"

"Again, I had no choice. I had to. It was either me or them."

The man's eyes remained like glass.

"I'm supposed to do something else here besides meeting you," she prompted.

"It has to do with this little trading post." He pointed in the store's direction. The three strolled over towards it. They spoke no words until they got closer.

"The man who runs it, I think he's a killer. He killed a little girl's family, maybe other traveling families. I need to get this little girl to the Nations to meet her uncle. Not sure if I can ride with you."

They lingered behind a tree line, still not in earshot of the trading post, while the man pondered her statement, spat on the ground again, and turned to Sara, "Who you taking with?"

"Just me, my friend, the Indian girl, and the little girl. She ain't but eight years old."

"You gonna need protection then from the LeRoux gang. Well, what's left of us."

"We'll ride with ya then. I have to get the kid and my friend. Let's see what's gonna happen in here. I'm supposed to walk in alone. You two can follow behind."

All three mounted their steeds and trotted towards the trading post. Not much happened down here. Some farmers traded supplies they would take home to feed their families and livestock. Nothing alarming as the three rode up. Another wagon rolled up, driven by an older black man. He dressed well, appeared distinguished, but never acknowledged the trio.

"Let's wait," Sara said to the two men.

"I agree. That man don't appear wicked, but in reality, I heard stories about him." The outlaw with a scar slashed across his face ran his hands through his bushy beard. His legs shook in his alligator skinned boots.

The boy froze, speechless. He might have seen a ghost, possibly one of his late father. Sara had a good idea who she was dealing with.

"Hell, he ain't nothing. Just showing his face to let me know everything is okay. We need to wait until he leaves." Sara took charge of the operation, something she'd regret. The outlaw, the machismo older man, gave in.

The colored man entered the shop. Not in a hurry to make any move, Sara and the two outlaws waited with the boy standing guard.

"Watcha know about that man?" Sara asked the scar-faced man.

"You know all about him. I saw it in your eyes and his eyes. Bet you saw in mine too."

"You made a deal with him?"

"Ah, Ms. Sara Barnum. Mon Pere has spoken about this man. Again, we must play it careful. Mon Pere gambled and lost once. This man likes his tricks. I was told by the man devil we must meet, and you and I must travel together, even before I saw you shoot that man. We can't go through Logansport. Too many witnesses to a massacre there. The one we caused."

"Not sure if we should go this way. The little girl's family got killed down by that home across that bayou." She pointed in the swamp's direction. "I'm not sure who lives there. Could be the man who runs this place."

"One way to find out." He pulled out his pistols and got to his feet. "Kid, get ready, we're going in."

Sara stared at the older outlaw, then at the kid, recognizing her God was on her side. Sara now had backups. She pushed to her feet and walked between the two men, her pistols loaded and in hand. Sara sighed as they approached the door. The older black man was still in the shop. She was could not tell if he made purchases, traded supplies, or set up a deal, but there was a reason he was there. Sara was certain there was a reason she met the outlaw gang as well, and there was a reason there were only two of the men. They walked in, Sara first, pushing the door open.

The old man appeared oblivious to the commotion that might ensue. He admired pelts that hung from the wall, leaning closer to peer at the gator skinned boots that sat on the shelf. A prodigy of his might have made them.

Mr. Grumbel watched the trio stroll up. Again, Sara led. The two outlaws flanked her side, both armed. The old man grabbed jars of peaches, turned around and smiled. He walked up to the counter, paid for his purchase, an eye still on Sara who retreated, still enveloped by the men.

The old man tipped his hat to the trio and walked out with the jars. The gang didn't acknowledge him in public. Mr. Grumbel reached down behind the counter to pull up a weapon, a small Colt he used to fend off robbers. "You're back with company, I see," Mr. Grumbel said. He stuttered and shook in his shoes. Six guns pointed straight at him.

"I know who you are, and what you've been doing, and even know where you live. You will not stop me from getting the little girl you left across Texas. I can turn you in, but there's a reward for me, and a reward for these boys here. You be responsible for all those killings along here? Well, you've butchered your last family, and you left one. I'm coming back with the witness. You better be here. These two men will make sure of that." Sara packed her pistols back in the holsters and walked out. Her two new partners remained behind.

While Sara rode off into the bayou, heading back to the Caddo, the man and the boy followed Mr. Grumbel to his home to better keep a watchful eye on him. The man did not appear spooked. He spent time with his wife and family, never letting on the secret to his household.

The outlaws heard his brother ride up, but remained hidden. They wanted to hear the conversation.

"I found Frank. He's dead, shot in the back. Folks said some girl was riding around, must have chased him down. Three outlaws in town chased the girl. I bet they took care of her." Silence, then the brother continued. "If she's dead, we might have to put this on hold for a while. That way, people can continue blaming it on her."

The younger outlaw snickered at the foolish thoughts of the serial killer. "Shall we go in?" he asked his partner. "Pistols pointed? You know, to scare da shit out of them."

The older man, who only smiled when expecting harm, lifted the brim of his black hat to expose his glass eyes. A sinister smile appeared on his face. He liked torture, and now another man could share the humiliation.

The two men walked into the Grumbel house, pistols in hand. The older man looked at the kid, cleared his throat to get the family's attention, and a cue for the boy to speak.

"The girl ain't dead. She's still riding. And guess who she's riding with?" He twirled the pistol on his finger. It did two revolutions and ended up pointed at the shopkeeper. "By the way, she has a witness with her as well, and will pass through tomorrow to meet us. So, you know what will be good for you." The gun swept through to point at the shopkeeper's brother. "You ain't gonna say nothing."

The brother was fortunate to confess to Jack LeRoux; the notorious man wanted across Louisiana and Texas. Jack LeRoux wasn't turning anyone in, since he was a cold-blooded killer himself. One sudden move and the Grumbel family would be on the floor, with blood spilling from their bodies. They would never be found guilty of their heinous crimes, but right that minute, they settled into a conundrum. Hell was waiting once the first family received their butchering. Taking out the LeRoux gang would not be easy. Both brothers were not about to make any false move, not even reaching for a weapon, as that would mean their end. Their only option left would be their intelligence and take advantage of any opportunity the gang left ajar. Louisiana outlaws weren't supposed to be the brightest unless they had divine intervention.

That evening, the LcRoux gang stayed inside the Grumbel residence waiting for the shopkeeper to return to his store. There they would meet Sara, Kaydence, and Rose.

Chapter 17

The girls were off before sunrise.

"I'm leading the way. Rose, you be riding with Kaydence. We're gonna go see your family. Our escort is the baddest man in Texas. Even the law is afraid of him. We be across Texas in two leg shakes."

She stood, arms folded, head bent, staring at the ground, refusing to get on with Kaydence. The protrusion on her lips was visible. "I wanna stay here." She slammed her foot into the Louisiana mud.

Kaydence hovered beside her bay pony, saddle bag packed full of her and Rose's gear. "Rose, we have to go. You can take the reins, while I teach you how to ride."

The little girl stole a glance at Kaydence. A slight smile emerged, then disintegrated as fast it appeared. She lowered her head. They needed a back-up plan.

They stood by the ashes of the campfire. The morning sun rose in the east, casting a warmth on the spring day. Sara pulled her hat down over her face, hiding the squished lips that showed when frustrated. She paced, looking towards the sunrise, hoping her God would grant her wisdom. A ruffle flew through the trees, and it wasn't the elves. Sara tipped her hat, then put it on straight.

"Rose, get with Kaydence, so she can teach you to ride." Sarah whipped out a pistol from her holster, leveled it at a hopping rabbit and fired once. She held the pistol close to her lips, blowing the smoke away. "I'll teach you to shoot like me. It ain't that hard. It just takes practice."

Rose's eyes lit up. Both girls knew little Rose wanted to ride, probably rope too, and that might be why they headed to Tulsa. Her uncle owned a ranch there and was a cattleman. He needed a lot of help and finding excellent help in the plains was tough sometimes. It required more than a family. A cluster of trusting people, whether it was employing transits or migrants, they all had to work together for a common cause, and that cause was Rose's uncle's wealth. He would compensate.

Sara and Kaydence aided Rose on to the horse. They felt safe as she took the reins. Sara mounted her steed and led the way. She and Papa galloped out of the commune towards the trail that led towards the store. There the three would meet the Leroux gang to become a makeshift gang of five, one a hardened criminal, one a youthful sidekick, a twenty-something woman, an older teenage girl, and an eight-year-old. All but Mr. LeRoux looked innocent enough. Outlawing would not be a priority, but survival was. That's how one becomes an outlaw in the Wild West. It was survival of the fittest, or baddest. Surviving is how Sara became an outlaw. She wondered about Jack Leroux.

Rose didn't do a terrible job riding the horse. She slowed the crew down a bit, such that they spent most of the time trotting. Kaydence grabbed the reins from her countless times to increase speed. About fifteen miles into the journey, they stopped for a break, despite they were losing time. Sara and Kaydence built a small, dainty fire, perfect to cook a few rabbits. While the flames burst into the daylight, Kaydence picked berries, while Sara took Rose out for her shooting lessons, her twenty-gauge Remington shotgun and rifle in hand. Rose would handle the shotgun. Training would be similar. Aim and shoot.

They hunted rabbits or squirrels, anything they could snag a quick meal from, grab some furs if needed. They wouldn't be trading the pelts with the trader.

"Okay, Rose, lay down on all fours on your belly."

Rose splatted in the dirt; her extended arms holding the shotgun almost in the proper position. Sara, patient as a tortoise chasing a cottonmouth in the swamps, eyed the youngster.

"No, you're holding da thing wrong. Here, watch me."

Sara sprawled down in the mud; her left arm bent at a ninety-degree angle. She set the barrel of the rifle between her thumb and forefinger, pointing at the trees. The butt of the gun pressed firm against her shoulder.

"See how I'm holding this. All you gotta do is move it around a bit." Rose adjusted her grip on the smaller gauged gun. She pointed it towards a clearing between the trees. "Close your left eye, look through the sight. It helps you focus on the target. Place your finger on the trigger. Use your pointer. Yeah, you got it. When you see a hare in your sight, pull da trigger. I'll be watching for one as well.

Rose aimed, waiting for a bunny to cross her path. Sara saw one first. She hollered for the girl to pull the trigger. Rose pulled it. A hare flew up in the air and went backwards a few yards. "I got it."

"Sure did. We got us some lunch, first shot as well. Let's go get it and I'll show you how to skin it, save the fur, if possible. If not, some critter will eat it."

They both hurried over to pick up the dead cottontail. 'Ah, the furs ruined, shot up too much, but we got some meat. This should feed the three of us. Let's go clean it up. You can watch me if you want. It's gross, but if you hunt stuff, you got to learn to clean it up."

The two girls followed the critters to the water's edge, crossing tree roots, fallen sticks and hiking through the mud, scared snakes scooting towards the stream. Sara filled up a basin with stream water and then set about to wash her knife and the bunny.

Kaydence strolled over, whistling an old Caddo tune while supervising the action. The hare cleaned down to the meat and bones, organs and fur tossed into the woods, and the trio grilled the rabbit and ate the berries Kaydence picked. The lunch was decent. After a few more rounds of shooting to enable Sara to ensure it wasn't beginner's luck for Rose, she missed all the targets Sara displayed, and then they ventured off to the trading post.

Once again Sara led the way, while Kaydence followed, taking the reins, unsure of what may lie ahead. The miniscule LeRoux gang, led by Jack LeRoux and his young partner Paul Ledbetter, waited for them. In their grasp was the possible serial killer and butcherer of Rose's parents. Evasive action might be needed, and Rose, still unskilled at maneuvering the equine through a bayou, clung to Kaydence's belly.

Through the clearing, they noticed the trading shop. Two horses, covered with packed saddle bags and fancy saddles, sat outside, tied at a hitching post, lapping up water from a wooden trough. They led the horses near the water station, dismounted, and led their steeds in for a drink. Kaydence grabbed the rope Rose tossed at her and displayed Caddo knot tying methods that even Sara was unaware of. Rose practiced looping the rope around. She tightened the knot, but not enough to choke the horse.

Sara strode towards the post. As she passed a wanted poster of her displayed on the store's window, she swiped it off the window. She held up the paper, admiring the artistry of the sketch, and then slammed the doors open. Jack LeRoux and Paul Ledbetter were not to be seen anywhere. Dallas Grumbel stood alone behind the counter. His free hand twirled the curls of his moustache. The other hand stayed hidden beneath the counter. Sara assumed he held a pistol. She was armed, two loaded pistols, and bullets stocked in her belt.

Eyeing Mr. Grumbel, she reached into her pocket and whipped out a thin cigar. She preferred the aroma and flavor induced by the corncob, with the essence of the Louisiana grown tobacco exiting the pipe. Smoking the tobacco-wrapped skinny cigar made her feel masculine, like she would take on all comers. They calmed her just enough not to do anything irrational.

She stuck the stogie in her mouth, grabbed a match, and struck the phosphorous tip of the flint. She sucked the smoke, exhaling it into the shop. "Where are the two men?" She eyed Mr. Grumbel, an older, scar-faced man, "and some young kid?" She approached the man with a methodical pace, not taking her eyes off him. Glaring at the man, she smoked with one hand, the other hand hanging near the pistol. "Where are they? Their horses are out front." Her hand inched closer to the pistol. She sucked in another puff and exhaled towards the shopkeeper.

Dallas Grumbel had a fair idea the girl traveled with the orphan child of one family he destroyed. He studied her face and the movement of her hand, while his remained hidden, concealing the weapon he possessed. Trusting in his experience with a revolver, and unaware of the girl's, he was certain he had an advantage. Knowledge of the location of the two outlaws again aided his leverage. Jack LeRoux and Paul Ledbetter remained in the post's cellar, hidden amongst snakes. The wisest man in the area, the shopkeeper, set a trap that the outlaws walked into. Frank Grumbel sat below in the damp, shallow storage facility.

Kaydence and Rose, on a hunch from a man above, refrained from entering the shop. Instead, they paced around the general store.

Rose kept her mouth shut as the two youngest members of the gang crept around the outside of the trading post. Kaydence noticed the cellar door first and the large footprints in the hardened mud. It appeared bodies were drug through the flattened weeds.

"Rose," Kaydence whispered. "Go into the store and let Sara know I'm going into the cellar. Drag her back here. Tell her you got to go pee or something."

Rose nodded, her blonde hair swishing in the Louisiana breeze. "One more thing, be quiet. Walk in the store. We need to be extra careful."

Rose crept around the shop corner, then turned and picked up the pace as she walked to the adjacent side. She really needed to relieve herself but kept walking, legs close together as if she walked on a sheet of ice. Her head bobbed back and forth, checking for danger. At the door, she caught Sara and Mr. Grumbel in a stare down, with their right arms down near their holster.

Little Rose transformed back to the spoiled little girl; the youngest child protected by her family, as she walked towards Sara. Dallas Grumbel reached for his weapon but relaxed as Rose whispered to Sara. "What she saying?" "I gotta take her in the back to pee. Dis little girl ain't made for country life. I just drop and squat, and I'm sure you'd love to see that." Her right hand stayed clenched near the holster.

"I'm coming with you. I don't want no sneaking off."

"You coming to watch a little girl pee? Are you a sicko? You not hiding nothing, are you?" She pulled the revolver out of the holster. "You're staying here. You come out, you're a dead man." She fired to miss, but she shot up a whiskey bottle on the back counter. Alcohol dripped onto the floor. "Next time I won't miss."

The man stayed behind the counter. There was no reason for him to think about a cellar attack. He did not know about the Indian girl breaking in from outside. He kept a suspicious eye on the girls as they walked out, and then followed them to the door, which was not unusual as Sara led the girl around the corner.

"I really have to pee."

"Drop and squat. Any idea where Kaydence is?"

Behind the shop, they found Kaydence finagling with the cellar storage doors. Sara stormed up to her.

"Take Rose inside and grab your gun. I'll get Paul and LeRoux out of there." Sara spoke like she had no care who heard her. "Let's pry these doors open, and have the revolver out, ready to fire."

She crawled into the cellar, kicked a storage door in with her boots, and saw the outlaw and the kid tied up. A fat man armed with a revolver stared at them. Sara barged in; pistol aimed at the fat brother's chest. "Do you want to cut the rope, or you want me to?"

"No need." the thick, husky voice rang out. Jack LeRoux already freed his hands and cut his partner's rope. They outnumbered Frank. "I'll take over, young lady." He wrestled the gun from the obese brother. It fell and Paul retrieved the weapon. "Lead us into the store."

The ground seems to shake as Frank went towards the stairs that led up to the shop. Now he was unarmed and followed by three known killers who had restocked their weapons. The dumber brother lifted the cellar door and climbed the steps.

"D-D-Dallas. They got free." Frank stuttered.

Kaydence was close enough to Dallas Grumbel. Any hesitation or reaction on his part would give her full control. He turned his head towards his brother. Kaydence chopped the gun from his hand and gained control. Rose stood by the door; her shadow looming tall. She shook like the pecan trees the general store sat nestled in.

Sara took over the conversation. "We asked to let us be. There are rewards out for us, but I know your secret. You are going down. We're gonna take you to the sheriff."

"We wanted men, big time," Jack LeRoux interrupted her. "You help me haul them in, then vanish. I'll probably be thrown in jail too, since I got me this nice little drawing of me." She uncrumpled the paper. "Not sure what counts more, a little light-skinned mixed girl, or the infamous Grumbel killers. Anyways, you can bust me out if needed."

The two brothers, still tied up, got tossed in the back of the carriage that Dallas Grumbel drove. Jack and Paul hooked their horses to the poles. Rose rode with Jack up front, while Paul kept a weapon trained on the two. Sara and Kaydence rode off, the sun setting on the West Louisiana skyline near the town of Many, where the sheriff's office sat. They arrived short of town in a couple of hours. The two men and Sara changed places, and she drove the buggy straight to the sheriff.

"Sir, I think you may want these men. They have been out there killing innocent families traveling through. I got me a survivor waiting, one family's kids I rescued." The sheriff sat smoking a less than aromatic cigar. Sara waved to blow the smoke away. Kaydence and Rose waited outside; the outlaws hidden out of sight.

Rose soon entered the office. "Sir, these men killed my family on our way to Tulsa. Daddy wanted to strike it rich in oil with his brother. We came from Georgia."

"I heard rumors about missing people." He exhaled a smoke ring, glanced at the wanted posters, and noticed a resemblance. He looked straight at Sara. "You wanted too, missy. Got three charges on you." He puffed on his cigar and looked at her accomplice. "You, Injun, are you taking care of this girl? Heard you Coushatta's up yonder are at peace?"

"Yes, my family is taking care of her. But some of my family is up in the territories. We might take her up there soon. Once   things   get   safer."
"We?" The man laughed. "You ain't going nowhere, but in dat cell over yonder. At least you won't be in here with these good   folk."
"I caught these so-called good folks. They killed at least one family. I can't be in the same jail as them."

The sheriff grabbed Sara's arms, confiscated her weapons, and cuffed her. He led her to a cell. In another cell, he drug the two brothers and spoke with them.

Sara could not make out what they were saying. She sat on the dirt floor, already incarcerated too long. The man wearing the shiny badge returned with a smile and walked into her cell.

"You in luck, those boys confessed. There is still a reward out for you. I'm getting with da law down in Baton Rouge to have them boys sent away. Meanwhile, gotta figure out what to do with you."

Some white men came and took the Grumbel Brothers away the next day. Sara hoped they were sent somewhere distant, but then again, she was in Louisiana. She wasn't sure what happened to them. Meanwhile, she sat in the jail, locked up, for one night, and then another. It was too many nights too long sitting in the cell. She needed to make a break.

Part II

Chapter 18

Sara heard a lonesome guitar play a tune, a song she had never heard before. The ditty haunted her, like ghosts rising in the bayous. Most people run from the noises, however the sound intrigued Sara. Her eyes raced back and forth as she jumped off the concrete bench, which served as her bed, to peer out the cell window. Through the bars of the jail window, she peeped at the stars and quarter moon. Clouds drifted by, covering up the earth's satellite, then drifted past. The stars beckoned, infatuated with the distant suns, while she kept track of them in her head. The song boomed louder, still unrecognizable. She saw no one playing, just heard the lone guitar being picked. Someone called for her.

The deputy slept in his chair, his feet on his desk. The ten-gallon hat he wore was pulled over his eyes. His snore was the lone sound in the small cell. She glanced around. Only a kerosene lamp illuminated the room. The deputy had hung them it up on the east wall. The rope she had been piecing together neared completion. She pondered hooking the keys to the tip of the rope and all she needed was to add a clasp. Sara needed a better escape strategy.

She retreated to the bench, her head in her hands, thinking. Another voice spoke, not the one playing guitar. This one was different, however hauntingly familiar. "You have feminine charms. Use them," the voice whispered in her ear, seductive, maybe to enhance her.

Sara, already twenty-two, had never pursued a man before, nor had a guy romanced her. The sole interest she had from males was ferry-boat operators she shot dead. Clueless on making herself desirable to the young deputy, she pondered other more intelligent ideas.

The man's voice kept speaking. "You have charms, all women do. It's the only way out. Your group needs you."

She shook her head. The guitar played louder. The song, beautiful and seductive. She knew it was time.

Still naïve on how this seduction thing worked, she didn't intend to kiss the sleeping kid, only to woo him in the cell with her devilish or siren charms, whichever was planted within her by the spirit. She spoke to it what she said no one knew,and his response would become her course of action.

"Deputy, oh deputy," she called in a soft voice. She adjusted her top, swished her hair back, hoping to awake the older teenager.

"Deputy Bourgeois," she called again, her voice throatier, more seductive than before. "How long am I gonna be in here? You know I ain't never kissed a man before. I'm hoping I'll kiss someone before they put me away. Maybe do some more stuff. It would be a shame to get hanged and never do stuff with a strapping young man." She stood by the door, hoping to arouse him from slumber.

The boy stirred in his sleep. Mumbling came from under the ten-gallon hat. He still slept, however, his hand moved toward his lap. Through the flickering light, Sara noticed the kid's arousal. She hoped he awoke soon. Satisfying his lust was the last thing on her mind.

She called again. "CJ Bourgeois, I know you can hear me, it's just you and me in the cell. If you don't say nothing, I won't tell." She untucked her prison garb, hoping to make her clothes a little more appealing to the male eye. "Come on, my stallion."

The deputy glanced over at the woman standing in the shadow as the light from the kerosene lantern flickered throughout the cell. She looked sultry; her hair hung down past her shoulders. When she shook her head, the hair swished in the breeze. He stood up and strolled towards her bow legged. He fumbled for the key as Sara retreated toward the bench of the cell. Her eyes focused on the young man, no longer interested in what he had under his jeans, but what he fumbled for on his belt, and that was the keys to her cell.

As the man inserted the key into the lock, Sara relaxed a second, releasing a deep breath.

He strode in towards her, taking no precautions, bow legged still. She walked towards him, her arms around him as they danced.

"I want a little dancing before I romance," she whispered in his ear. "We're all alone, together, deputy." She retreated a few steps, clapped her hands, stomped her feet to the music in her head. A fiddle replaced the guitar tone. She did a jig as they hooked arms on the elbow. They twirled, stepped back, stomped their feet, and kicked up their heels. She doubted he heard the music, but he kept rhythm with her. He wasn't a terrible dancer. They spun a few times, then skirted across the mud prison floor, from the cell window to the open door. Then they skipped back across the saturated dirt towards the outside window.

She pressed her tight body against him. He became a gentleman attempting to romance her. She peered through the open window, marred only by the cell bars. She stared at the sky; aware the bounty would chase her through the night.

"I mean, I don't care whenever you come around, you're so strong." She massaged his bicep, and in a softer but huskier voice, cooed in his ear. "I've been thinking about you all night, been wanting to give you my first kiss."

He leaned in to kiss her. She didn't turn away, taking a chance he might not notice her hands reaching for the belt that contained the keys, his revolver and several bullets. She continued the torturous wrath of his lips. The boy, a terrible kisser, had no seduction skills.

Sara fumbled until she finally pulled his belt off him, grabbed the pistol, checked to see if it was loaded, then pointed it at the man. "Go to the window, put your hands on the bars." She unlocked the cuffs, clamping him to the cell window. All he could do was peer out at the moonlight.

"Keep your trap shut. I can shoot ya from in here or out there." She pointed the revolver towards the window she attached his hands to. Firing a shot would bring attention. Sara slammed and locked the cell door, grabbed her rifle and the rest of her belongings, before slipping out the front door with the deputy's keys and pistol. She snuck around to the back, where the barred window lay with a sheriff's deputy clamped to it. She cocked the pistol, pointing it at his face, which dripped with perspiration.

"I know where you're spending the night, not sure where I might be, but it might be close. If I hear ya call out, you will dangle from these cuffs with a pool of blood waiting for ya."

Nothing and no one waited for her outside. The gang must have snuck into the bayou with her horse, and the rest of her possessions. She stripped out of the prison garb, tossed on the clothes she rode in on. After packing the shapeless attire, they provided her, she ran towards the swamp, no longer hearing the guitar plucking. She had to find her group.

Following the quarter-moon, she strode through the bayou, not caring about the crawling reptiles that could take her down with one chomp. Sara intensified her pace, sprinting through the thicket, hiding in the cane-breaks, listening for the saddened tone of a guitar to guide her way. She heard nothing but hummed the ditty she listened to in the cell. Acknowledging the tune would lead her to her crew.

She stopped her trek for a few minutes to catch her breath, exhaling several times. She glanced around. The moon had snuck behind the clouds, leaving nothing to see but darkness and a few stars the clouds refused to cover. She grabbed her knees, and with her head bent over, she thought she heard a dog barking. Sara pondered the idea that the deputy might have somehow freed himself and sent a posse after her. After one more deep breath, she gathered herself and sprinted towards the river. Squishing snakes along the way, she meandered through the bayou. Finally arriving at a clearing, the moon broke free from the cloud cover. She saw its descent in the western sky. Morning was coming, the posse would become closer. Horses moved faster than a young lady can run.

The barking grew louder. The night sky soon replaced with a slight brightness behind her. Kneeling over, she searched west. The sky had turned an evil orange, while the giant star broke free from the horizon behind her. The posse was close enough for human voices to be heard, but not made out. She had enough strength for one more sprint. The haunting guitar returned. She smiled, acknowledging the meaning of the music. Sara didn't know if the song was in her head, or someone sat picking a six string for her. She bolted for the harmonic tones of the eerie guitar, making out a hymn she recognized from her youth in Colfax. "Yes, we'll we gather at the river, the beautiful, the beautiful river. Gather with saints at the river that flows with the grace of God."

Safety was near. She hoped her tired legs would sustain for the next mile or so as she jogged towards the bank of the river. The gospel hymn became louder. The dogs' barking amplified. She continued darting across the fields, but another bayou guarded the Sabine. This one was thick and dark. The river sat on the other side, so sat Texas and freedom from the Louisiana law.

She no longer heard the voices. The hound's yaps vanished as well, while a Caddo chant replaced the hymn. Sara sat, pondering how to navigate the thick reptile infested, muddy-bottomed bayou. She stared at the ground saturated with overflow from the river. As her feet sank into the ground, she snuck through. She descended by a few inches and sought a dryer path to cross. Towards the north, she spotted an easier method and navigated through the shallow water. Her legs becoming weaker as she trudged through. A small island, an oasis in the bayou, sat towards the south. She crawled through the swamp onto dry but muddy land.

Silence surrounded Sara as she sat in a thick grove of cypress trees. No howling of hounds, no guitar picking, no hymns to guide her. Her legs refused to go any further. The river had to be near, but she sat stuck, tired with no food, no drinking water.

Egrets flew by, she saw alligators cruise through the shallow swamp searching for their morning meal. Croaking bullfrogs broke the silence of the swamp, while bass searched for the frogs to fatten themselves up for the gators. She crawled around her little private island, searching for a safe shelter. She crawled into a dug-out cypress, pulling her hat over her head, as her body required food, hydration and rest.

She woke up to the gentle hiss of a water moccasin, upset its home had been invaded. Her knife was always ready, and with a quick but steady movement, she slashed towards the hiss and plunged it deep into the skull. The snake lay dead.

The sweet southern song vanished, as the morning light shone brightly, her only guiding light in the thick bayou. No longer able to hear the splash of the river, no fiddles, guitars or harmonicas blowing, her stomach rumbled and growled. Her throat felt dry, since she had quenched nothing. Sneaking out of the cypress, no sounds but her own body. Staring again at the sky, she noticed the sun had disappeared behind the clouds. After her brief nap, she made her way through the bayou. Sara knew how to kill a gator if needed. She made her way west. The swamp cleared; cotton fields spread out across the valley. The sun emerged behind her in the Eastern sky.

She glanced around, making sure they had not spotted her laying in the field. The cotton stood tall enough where she'd never be discovered, at least by humans. Humans had dogs; dogs were good sniffers. She sat, attempting relaxation, waiting for the lonesome song that influenced her escape. She covered her eyes, ignoring the snakes, Bo weevils and other creatures that scattered past her.

She didn't know what she heard first, the lonesome song, this time accompanied by a mandolin break and banjo thumping. Her ears perked up like a canine's, but she heard the barking of hounds. The music came from the west, the hounds to the east, and Sara knew which way to run. Keeping low, she cut through the plantation and scampered as fast as possible.

Soon, she arrived at a large home with burned out shacks and tree line surrounding it. The home, plantation style, she assumed was owned by someone who would lynch her, claim the reward money, and sell her decapitated body to the press for pictures of his capture, increasing his fortune. She ducked back into the fields. Her thoughts needed recaptured. The southern song in her head disappeared. The howling of the hounds increased.

She scanned the burned-out shacks behind the home and moved north in the fields, trampling the crops without a care about some cotton farmers' money. Survival was the sole important decision in her life. She approached the north end of the field and heard the song play again, this time a fiddle and harmonica joined other instruments in a five-part harmony. The song came clear as day from a shack, burnt but still standing.

The plantation home stood in clear view; while the shack nestled back in the grove as the hounds' barks grew louder. They picked up her scent, but were still back, plus she could outrun men holding the canines. The house looked empty, or no one must have been awake, or breakfast was about to be eaten. She dashed a half-mile across the open field, crashing through the door to the vacant shack inside. The music stopped. Sara spotted a small opening, crawled through on all fours, and stood tall as a tree. She glanced into the bayou, as the song came to her again. She guessed the Sabine flowed near since the aromas surrounding her turned musky. Zigzagging her way through the trees, the song soon replaced by a raging gushing river, Sara sprinted towards the Sabine, her hair flying back. She maintained her possessions until she found sitting on the shore, a skiff, a dugout canoe, one that looked like the Caddo used for fishing.

Across the river, she noticed two girls, Kaydence, Rose, and a young man with a guitar, Paul. He sat, plucking the strings under a pecan tree. Jack LeRoux vanished. Sara paddled the skiff across the raging river, the current moving her further south than intended.

Chapter 19

T he tune the lanky youth picked under the trees in the East Texas bayou sounded nothing like the song Sara heard guiding her to her crew. He glanced up, noticed the girls struggling with the skiff, and rested his guitar next to a tree. He sprinted towards her expected landfall.

Sara struggled with the boat. The fast channel on the west end of the river kept pushing her downstream. She paddled against the current, moving the watercraft north.

"Throw me the rope." Paul yelled to her.

Rose and Kaydence joined Paul on realizing that the youth needed help in hauling the boat in. The rope flew towards shore to land at Paul's feet. He tugged, and with the aid of the two younger girls, pulled Sara ashore.

"You like my guitar, Ms. Sara?" Paul asked, reaching down to pick it up from the tree. The tree had an eerie resemblance to what Sara noticed earlier in her adventures.

"Yeah, where did you get it? I didn't see it with you before." Her curiosity intensified.

"Some old man dropped it off by this tree. He fiddled with these here nobs at the end, then he took off. Jack followed him out of here, and said he was scouting a trail for us to get to Tulsa and that it's going to be a long haul. We were coming back to get you. Guess we don't have to. So, you broke out?"

"Yeah, I had to use my feminine charms, but I made it. I followed the music." She peered up at the young man. "I liked what I heard, so I kept running towards the picking." She plopped on the mud next to the bank. Rose joined her, while Kaydence climbed into the skiff, hauling the bag she ran across Western Louisiana with.

"Feminine charms?" He snickered and glanced the girl over and noticed her a little different, recognizing the young woman in her. He grabbed her hand, lifted her up to her feet, and they strolled towards the forest, away from the exposed riverbank. Kaydence pushed the skiff back into the rapid flowing river. She stepped back to watch it flow downstream, hoping for a capsize that would help destroy evidence. She joined her crew into the West Texas bayou from where they heard the hounds barking on the Louisiana side, while making their way for a safe dinner and rest.

Sara's pony waited. Papa recognized her voice and went back to search for grass to chew and grab a slurp of water. The other horses paid no attention as the foursome strolled up to where they camped in a small clearing, near a stream a few hundred yards west of the Sabine. The trail that went north was where Jack LeRoux made his way.

After a dinner of fish and berries, they gathered around the fire. Paul found a place next to a tree. He picked up his guitar, picked some old hymns, and the others joined in four-part harmony. Rose sang the loudest. She sang those songs every Sunday back home in Savanna, Georgia.

"Can you play something else?" Kaydence looked at Paul, her brown eyes gleamed, she looked like a girl infatuated with a boy, the way her eyes roamed over him.

Sara watched Kaydence stroll towards him. "I can teach you some songs we sang at night." Her eyes kept their glow, enveloping his tall, string bean body.

Sara noticed the infatuation her younger friend had for the teenager. Some cardinals flew by and crossed the river. Paul quit playing but held on to his guitar. Kaydence sang a song the shaman taught her called Redbird.

"Sing it for me, baby, and I'll try to follow along." Paul wet his lips like he wanted to steal a kiss from the young Indian girl.

She sang a verse in Caddo, first, while Paul tapped along on the mahogany wood of his guitar, making a light drum sound.

"Redbird, redbird
He got scared, he flew up out of the bush.
It must be getting close to daylight."

The bright ball rose from the eastern sky, reflecting a pretty portrait over the river. The cardinal flew past them again.

"We have to get going," Kaydence announced.

Sara packed her bag and went out to stroke her horse. It had been a week since she rode Papa, and both horse and rider missed each other. She wanted to get moving. Kaydence, after watching the birds fly across the river, knew the bounty was aware of their whereabouts. Paul, wise for his age, paid attention and listened to the women.

All three in harmony shouted to the girl. "C'mon, Rose, we got to roll along."

The harmonies of their voices were sweet, but assertive came with a musical tone. Rose, young, naïve, but learning the outlaw way, struggled to her feet. Stumbling and tripping over a tree root, she crawled towards her horse. They heard the hounds and spotted them through the groves. Several white men, the bounty hunters, as well as sheriff's deputies stood on the river's edge, hollering at the fugitive youths, but the renegades never made out the voices.

"Those cardinals either warned us or gave away our hiding place." Paul checked the campfire. It no longer burned, no sparks, no embers, everything a gray ash color. They needed to roll out.

Rose struggled to straddle her pony.

"C'mon Rose, we need to roll, we need to roll along, if we gonna get you up to the Cimarron to visit your uncle."

"This horse is too big for me right now." She kicked the ground, startling the pony. It whinnied and kicked up. Sara soothed it with her touch and aided Rose to the saddle.

"Jack took that trail over yonder." Kaydence pointed to a clearing northwest. "I'm not sure about it." She pointed to a thinner clearing towards west. "This is the one I think takes her home. Let's take this trail. Not sure about that pistolero, anyway."

Kaydence had the sixth sense required. Sara knew Jack, and she made a deal with the same God. She knew that God represented the devil, and she witnessed Jack LeRoux gun down townspeople over in Logansport. The devil can protect or betray you. Someone well versed Sara on the makings of the man LeRoux dealt with. Once you betray Legba, anything could happen. She agreed to take the alternate trail.

"There will be no crime against the people on this journey. No crime against the people." The voice echoed through Jack LeRoux's head as he approached the steel rails.

The Texas Pacific crossed from Shreveport to Dallas. In the muck of Northeast Texas, Longview was a popular destination. In Marshall, it already bore the thick whiskered outlaw traveling with the youths. He cut his snuff off with his knife and whipped a chunk into his mouth. A kick from his spurred boots sent the saloon door flying open,while his eyes pondered the tavern. Jack, well known in these parts of the woods, searched for a friendly face. He sought one who refused to challenge and refused to run. None of the cowboys whipped their revolvers out. A group seated at the bar never raised their eyes from the bottom of their amber whiskey glasses. At a table in the corner, the men never raised their faces, too busy concentrating on their aces, flushes, or whatever cards they held. The bartender knew Jack Leroux, the gunfighter, a good customer who spent money renting a whore and tipped her good. The man running the saloon knew his reputation outside the bar as well. He kept acknowledged the gunslinger.

The whores in the saloon glanced over at the poker players but were ignored. Then the group of bosomy women, some brunette, one blonde, and a mixed-race woman, wondered over to a group of scrawny boys about Paul's age. LeRoux watched them, eyed their seduction technique at seducing seventeen-year-old boys who were selling ice to a rice farmer in the Delta.

Like a hawk, LeRoux watched the young whores float over to the gangly kids, attempting to drown their loneliness with shots of whiskey. The three boys, farm kids, green to Texas, ran away from their Indiana home, combined their money and bought a ticket to Texas. Marshall was the first stop. They had enough money for drinking. No fucking.

The whores received their free booze, sat on the boisterous kid's lap, taking off their cowboy hats, running their fingers through the youths' curly hair, to get them to drop a couple of bits to be taken upstairs for the night.

"We don't have that kind of money because we spent it all in here and on the train ticket. We're looking for work in the morning," the tallest, the one who seemed to be the oldest of the crew, told the mixed-race girl. She noticed Jack, whom she had serviced before. Jack smiled at the girl. She studied the snuff dripping onto his beard and smiled at him. Enticing the boy further, she rubbed her hand on his thigh.

The outlaw overheard the prostitute, "You have such sturdy legs. You must ride a lot. I bet those legs are powerful." She leaned in kiss his ear. She stared straight at the outlaw, winked, as he strolled over to the youths. Jack told the oldest kid to follow him.

"Tell ya what. I'll pay for us all to have a little fun here since I just got back, got some work to do at my ranch. I'll spot you some play money, if ya help me out tomorrow. Only thing is, I get this one for the night." He grabbed the mixed-race girl by the hand, and they waltzed across the barroom floor to an unheard music.

The other three women grabbed the boys and led them to the hotel rooms upstairs. Jack told the bartender.

"I set those boys for the night." He plopped another few bits on the counter for the tip.

"You must have knocked up some little place to get this kind of dough."

The outlaw smirked, smiled, and said nothing. He grabbed his lady's hand, and they disappeared up the steps into Marshall's sleaziest hotel.

Jack bought a few horses for the youths at a trading post that morning. He rode back to the hotel, where the kids enjoyed breakfast with the women. He peered over at the young men, watching them scoop down the last of the flapjacks and bacon. They saw him, got up, left the women, and hoping for another round that night, followed Jack LeRoux out the door.

They mounted the ponies.

"We're going to my place," he told the kids, waiting for them to settle in on their saddles. Jack Leroux had no home outside Marshall. He lived on the trails in Northeast Texas and Northwest Louisiana. He had connections all the way to Ft. Worth. The man was wanted and feared, but his protection across this region of the state was almost as large.

They rode out of town, heading west for a good five miles out of town. LeRoux knew the schedule of the train by heart. Again, bored with Paul and the girls, he craved entertainment. He didn't want to mess with Sara. She handled a gun way too good for a young woman. Besides, he wanted a woman's touch, not a younger woman's. The man had standards for carnal pleasures. He'd rather do a whore than a virgin.

Six miles west of town, they set up camp. The tree line stood at its thickest here. No one could spot them. "You boys wait here. Once I signal, you'll ride out on the tracks, praying the engineer and brakeman see you in time." He pulled both pistols out of the holster, aimed both weapons at both boys.

Their eyes widened in fear, too scared to protest. The tallest of the boys followed him. He required an assistant to steal from the passengers. He'd give them their share, ride on to Ft. Worth to give Mr. Bourgeois his share of the loot, and then ride back east to reunite with Sara and company near the Texas-Oklahoma border. This was his plan, anyway. It was against Legba's.

Riding back to the hideout, the oldest boy, the scheduled partner in the robbery, got brave. He talked back, making a fatal mistake. "I thought we were doing farm work. That's why we came out here. I don't wanna rob no train. We ain't trained robbers. It's against God's will. I'm refus..." He spoke no more. Shot off the horse, he laid on the tracks.

Jack got his horse in gear and rode to his brothers. He never liked witnesses. In a matter of seconds, the other two brothers lay dead upon the tracks, their Hoosier blood painting the steel rails crimson. He needed money for his protector. The alternate trail, the one he knew the youth would take, rode through Longview. He knew he could coax them.

Paul led the way, the girls behind him watching Paul's horse trot ahead of him.

"I'm glad that mean man is gone." Rose said to both girls.

"He ain't gone," Sara replied. She spat some loose-leaf tobacco juice in the mud. "He's gonna meet us somewhere. Where he meets us is anyone's guess. Next town we get to, someone but me gotta find us a map."

They rode North along an open trail; the horses trotting along the path. The dogs that trailed them had gone silent. Either the posse chasing them gave up, or they searched for a ferry crossing. Even if the latter, they gained considerable distance. No need to hurry, especially with Jack Leroux waiting somewhere up North.

A wagon trail crossed about fifteen miles into the trip. Paul halted the ride, allowing the three girls to catch up.

"This is the way to Logansport. Over there's a forest we could grab some grub." He put the field glasses to his eyes and peered over the horizon. "Looks like a trading post up yonder. We could get some critters here, trade them off for more supplies and a map. Not too far from this trail here, doubling back won't be that bad." He looked at Sara, his grin as wide as the valley they rode through. "Watcha think?"

Sara, impressed with the leadership qualities of the boy, smiled back. This was her ride though, and she knew the person in charge, and was relieved there was no Jack bossing the crew along. "These horses are pooped, need some water and rest. You say this is da road to Logansport. Ain't a ferry crossing over there?"

Paul looked over his shoulder towards the Eastern sky. "Yeah, that's right. Can't stay too long then. If that posse comes, it will be easy for the hounds to pick our trail."

Kaydence and Rose watched the duo like the hawks that circled above, almost like the birds spied for the posse, or Jack LeRoux.

Sara waited for Paul, who waited for the girl to decide. They stood gawking at each other, admiring the knowledge they each portrayed. Both chewed the tobacco, waiting for the other to spit. At that time, they would decide. Paul leaned first. A wad fell onto the trail, nailing a spider. Sara bent her head over, the spit targeting a scorpion.

Kaydence and Rose knew Paul would soon speak. He did, "Let's get these ponies some water. I don't need nothing; then let's mosey on up to da trading post over yonder. I don't think folks know me, even though I have been riding with Jack for a while. I'll take Rose with me. Sara and Kaydence, you just ride on past for a bit, hide out and wait. Most of these places don't like redskins or colored girls. We will be caught on the spot even if we weren't wanted for nothing." He looked at Rose. "There might be a wanted poster for me up here. I don't think they know me, but if there is, you need to see if you can get a map all by yourself. Just make something up."

Sara and Kaydence looked at each other, wondering what Jack LeRoux would do. They ventured behind the tree line; a small stream flowed down, eventually settling into the Sabine. The horses lapped up the brook water, stopped to chew some grass, while Sara and her misfit gang stretched their tired legs.

Sara rambled toward the boy. "I like the way you think. We might be excellent partners on this journey." She looked at him, no idea if she flirted or just wanted to give him a compliment.

He tipped his hat at her.

Smiling, she responded, "You make it easy. You're an ace out here on da run. I'm glad we got these other two with us. Might have a power struggle without dem with us. We'd be yelling   at   each   other   the   entire   time."

He grabbed her hand. She squeezed his back while they strolled away from the other two girls. They vanished a little deeper into the forest, hidden behind a thicker grove of pecan trees. Both of their cheeks widened by the tobacco, as they both looked like squirrels gathering acorns for winter. The trees thinned out; a gleam of sunlight shone through the thick forest. They both spat the wad of tobacco out at the same time.

"Not sure if I want any kissing or nothing else on this." She backed away from him, stumbling over a root of an oak tree.

His grin got bigger. He tapped his guitar hung over his back on the leather strap he made. "No one said anything about that until you just did. You must be thinking about it. Wish we were here longer. I wrote a song for you, when you were in da jail house for way too many nights. I'd like to play it for ya, but we must be running."

Sara's face grew a bright shade of red. Her secret revealed, and standing speechless for a second, mouth agape. In a nervous voice, she stuttered. "Yeah. Yo... you're r... right."

She felt weak for a minute. She turned ahead of the boy, refusing his hand as they journeyed back to the other two girls. The horses looked up at them, their hooves scratching the East Texas mud. The equine appeared bored already, but refreshed and fed. They wanted to roll. The humans did, too.

The trading post soon came into view with no visual aid. Sara and Kaydence kept riding. They settled a few yards off the main trail, adjacent to a small creek that sat a mile north of the trading post. They tied up the horses, wandered around, searching for squirrels, picking berries, and fruits of the trees.

"You like him?" Kaydence blurted out the question to Sara.

"I guess maybe, I mean, I don't know. I think he likes me. Why do ya ask?"

Kaydence sat on the ground with her back resting on the bark of a gigantic oak. "I kind of like him, but I think he thinks I'm too little. Plus, when you were in jail, he kissed me right here." She pointed to her lips. "I thought he loved me, then you came around again. He's ignoring me now."

"Well, we shouldn't be worried about that stuff. We need to get Rose up there by that Cimarron River, where her uncle lives. That's our primary concern. Ain't that by your people too?"

"Nah, my tribe ain't near Tulsa. I want to head back after we get her up to her family."

"Look, a rabbit," Sara said, and pointed her shotgun. The rabbit hopped, but she nailed it. "Look, another one." She aimed and got rabbits for both. "We need to get a couple of more or squirrel. Should be no problem. Lots of critters running around. Gonna make you kill the other critters. I'll start cleaning these and build a fire."

Kaydence strolled through the forest in search of varmints. She spotted a deer, a small buck with small antlers protruding about six inches through its head. She raised her rifle to her eye. The buck watched her, unaware of what was about to happen. His big brown eyes hypnotized Kaydence. Raised to hunt for food, clothing, blankets and everything else that a buck provided, she hesitated for a brief second. The buck kept his sympathetic look. Kaydence took a deep breath, not taking her eye off the animal, and then pulled the trigger. The kick of the rifle sent her back to the ground. The bullet had gone straight through the deer's heart.

"Sara," she yelled. "I got us something more than a rabbit. Come help me carry this thing. Don't want to scratch the hide. Might get us some cash later, and meals for the trip."

Sara ran over, saw the dead buck, and grinned. "Guess we will bunk here for the night." She observed the large critter laying in the pile of blood. "It would be better if we clean it here, move the camp here. Start cleaning it, and I'll douse the fire and ride near the trail to wait for Rose and Paul."

She hiked west towards the trail. Lifting the glasses to eyes, she peeked south and observed two horses galloping at full speed. The riders arrived soon enough, both out of breath. They steered the horses into the grove, pulling up on the reins to halt the equine. Sara mounted Paul's horse and sat behind him. Kaydence sat in the grove, slicing the deer up. Rabbits roasted on the fire. All four gathered around the campfire. The coals of the branches and logs burned down enough to cook the deer meat. Kaydence tended to the meal, letting Paul and Sara to finish butchering the stag.

Rose gasped for air.

"Take a deep breath," Paul ordered, head turned to help Sara with the slicing.

All but Kaydence finished their chores. She remained slicing up her kill.

Paul continued, "They were looking for me. Not you guys, but they said some little orphan girl might travel this direction heading north through the Nations towards Tulsa. I told them I needed to get to Austin, cause that's the only town I could think of on the spot. I asked the man which way to Austin, and he pointed towards it. We thanked them, walked out, got on the horses and rode around the shop, then got behind it and rode as fast as we could. Not sure if they followed us."

Paul's and Rose's horses wandered down to the stream to slurp up the water. Tired from the sprint, they attempted to dry the creek with their drinking. The initial deer steaks were done, they still had plenty of meat left, and a hide to ride with. "I'm thinking we need to get riding along." Sara told the group. "Don't want to waste this creature. It could feed us most of the way up." She looked at Paul. "Ya think they followed you two?"

He finished chewing the first bite of venison. "Not sure. I don't think so. Let's get enough jerky, get some rest. Maybe get this hide cleaned off and skedaddle right away." He opened the map. "The man showed us where Austin was. It's down here. If they follow us, they will go the wrong way." He pointed on the map towards Oklahoma. "This is the way we need to ride. This trail will take us up to Longview. We could settle down there for a couple of days."

"Okay, let's rest." Sara took over the conversation after slicing off a chunk of meat with her knife. She ate the flesh right off the blade. "Let's get this little buck ready, so we'll have food and get a good price for the hide at the next trading post." She rose and stretched her arms. "I'm going to go talk to my person. Them little private talks we have are like prayers. I hope he will be listening."

She strolled over to a little clearing. Two thin paths crossed each other, not wide enough for a wagon to pass through, but distinct in which way they went. She knew he would meet her here. "Not sure if these guys gonna follow us or not. We headed to Longview for a few days. We gonna rest up there. This is our plan." Sara pulled the hat over her eyes, whipped out a plug of perique tobacco, a flask of whiskey, and placed it on the muddy ground. The flask sunk a bit in the wet soil. She blew the smoke east towards the devil's home, pulling her hat over her eyes.

The sun moved from straight on top of them, heading west, afternoon turned into early evening. Paul stood above her with his guitar. The small flask of whiskey was now empty, as was her tobacco bag. She had more with her. She looked up at the boy with the guitar. His breath had a hint of tobacco with a splash of whiskey on it.

"You him?" she asked the kid. "That man is old and colored, but I heard his appearance can change."

"What man? I'm just a lonesome kid, an orphan, and I ain't no devil or nothing. I'm trying to find my way in this world." He sat beside her to light his pipe. The perique tobacco exited the bowl and floated to the sky. He settled the guitar around himself, stretched out to lie beside Sara, whose head rested against a tree trunk. Paul, with his guitar across his chest, his hands set in a picking position. They both stared at the sky.

"Is this a good time to play my new song?"
"Go ahead. I'm resting, been on the run forever it seems like. I have been running my entire life. Sometimes it's nice to stretch out, listen to a fire, or a banjo or guitar being strummed."

Paul picked at his guitar and the notes were simple, nothing the devil would cook up for him. He sang about the journey, and the girl he yearned for. It wasn't a love song, or song about lust. The lyrics were simple, written from the heart.

Oh, my lady, my little lady,

roaming the bayou
Running from glory, running from everything
Running from the law, running from me
Yet, she still wants me to sing.
I'll sing her a sad, sad song
When she rides along
At night she takes my hand
Leading me through Texas
To her promised land.

He repeated the lyrics, his gaze fixed on her. She pulled the hat down over her eyes and never looked up. His song seemed to relax her enough to fall asleep. Watching her sleep brought a smile to his face. His spiritual father was correct. He picked the right girl of the two. He plopped his guitar on the wet soil, stretched out beside her, and pulled his hat over his eyes. They slept in peace, varmints ignoring them to crawl through the forest.

Rose woke first. She walked to the creek, found a spot, and splashed water across her face. After bathing, she left the little creek dripping wet. Paul and Sara were still asleep. She didn't bother to wake them. It was still dark; the moon provided the lone light. She snuck back to the campsite she shared with Kaydence. She shook her partner. "I thought I heard something. We need to get moving. The guys from the store, I think they are coming."

"Where are Sara and Paul?" Kaydence peered around the campfire, taking a quick body count.

"They're over there". Rose pointed to the clearing, which could not be spotted because of the darkness. "I didn't want to wake them."

"Wake them, or disturb them? The tone came out crisper than Kaydence intended. Rose looked at her, stunned. She receded a few steps. "We can't go yet; I'm smoking this deer."

"I thought I heard something. Can't we leave the deer? I mean, coyotes eat deer, don't they?" Through the moonlight, Kaydence noticed Rose's body shook. She looked terrified.

"Did you have a dream, or was it a vision? I have visions, they tell me things. Not sure if Jesus gives you a vision." Kaydence got to her feet. She worked hard skinning and slicing the little stag. She didn't want to leave it for scavengers. It was bad luck not to use everything you kill. She ventured towards where Sara and Paul drifted off. She carried a torch, walking through the clearing and disappearing from Rose's view.

Sneaking through the forest with the light of a fire on the log, she noticed the bodies, and wandered towards the two. "We need to skedaddle. Rose heard something."

Sara and Paul both grumbled unintelligibly. They glanced at each other, smiling like lovers who enjoyed the carnal treasures of one another. They rose and Paul grabbed his gear. Sara snuck behind Kaydence. Paul followed the two oldest girls. Rose alone sat by the fire, shaking. All three listened to Sara.

"I know they are coming for us."

Paul and Sara glanced at each other. Each waited for the other to decide. In the flickering light from the campfire, both sets of eyes didn't budge from one another.

"Let's ride." Sara broke the ice.

They packed, with the light of the campfire leading the way. Rose still sat shaking, while the other three did the work. They packed what they could of the small buck, left a good chunk of flesh and the bones for scavengers. The campfire doused the four horses and their riders trotted out of the forest onto the trail. They trotted until daybreak. No one followed. And they put in a good ten miles. The sun rose in the eastern sky. The sleep they planned was interrupted by a screaming eight-year-old. Whether she heard something was anyone's guess. The new campsite in Rusk County was near the burgeoning community of Henderson. They snuck through the town, comprising several brick buildings along the dusty main street. They spotted a creek and followed it into the woods. There they set up camp, hoping to go undiscovered.

They desired a good day or two of rest before heading to Longview. In Longview, they'd clean up and search for alternate transportation north, possibly by train, maybe stage. None of them missed Jack LeRoux.

Resting in a small clearing, which became their home for the next two days, Kaydence took over tanning the deerskin she salvaged. Sara scouted the area in search of the posse chasing them. Paul laid back to pick tunes and stand guard. Rose observed all three, fascinated with the way this small team grew in a matter of a week.

Sara rode back and reported nothing. Paul mounted his steed, rode off towards town, and back again, reporting nothing out of the ordinary. Kaydence sliced the hide. She made moccasins and jackets for the foursome. The rest she'd trade in town to collect train fare.

Chapter 20

J ack sat in the Mobberly Hotel barroom. Not intending to make a move until his younger gang arrived, he hustled between Longview and Dallas, doing petty crimes, hustling pool halls, and cheating his way at cards to clear a few thousand dollars. Gone was the thick bushy beard and moustache. He was nearly unrecognizable, with a trimmed hairline and clean-shaven face. He sat at the bar and nursed his whiskey, sober for what was coming.

Soon he retired to his room. The fire in the fireplace flickered, the shadows giving off an eerie glow, reflecting the cherry wood furniture in the room. His whore he brought up to the room, a mulatto and drifter from East Texas or Louisiana like himself, settled in Longview in the Lone Star State searching for something. What she searched for was anyone's guess. It could not have been a blood-thirsty gunslinger. Tillie, the whore, met Jack a mere two nights earlier. They had been together ever since he stayed in town. He promised her matrimony, a stable life, and no more gunslinging or outlawing. He hadn't kept true on his promise.

Jack attempted becoming a man and turning over a new leaf. Did this woman plant a seed in him? A cheating gambler might be a better occupation than a blood thirsty gunslinger and train robber. Tillie knew nothing about his past. She saw a money roll and never asked where it came from.

As long as she got her money, she didn't mind, and as long as he got sex he craved, he cared less. He didn't love her. He had no clue of the meaning of the word.

Jack returned to the hotel bar to sip his whiskey, while Tillie wandered the saloon in search of potential clients. Jack kept a careful eye on her as she strolled across the saloon floor, avoiding dancers doing a reel, and barmaids hauling whiskey and beer. He had gotten his already, and any money she made was a bonus to him, so he didn't object.

Four youths wandered in. After selling a deer hide, they had money for a couple of rooms at Longview's finest hotel. Jack spotted the fugitives. The clothes they wore were caked in dirt and mud, the jeans ripped, and it looked like they hadn't bathed except in river water. Sara and company had been on the run for over a week. They planned on two nights to get rested for the remainder of the journey.

The place was more luxurious than the children expected. They marveled at the elegance. None of them had witnessed the extravagance of a place like this before. They turned and walked out, looking for something more suited to their upbringings. Their exit was undetected, except for the man wearing a black pants, white shirt with a vest. His short hair was slicked back, and he sat with a clean shave. He smiled.

The man walked out after the kids. He watched them search for a less lavish place to rest. They wandered past the railroad station, found a hitching post, tied the ponies up, and wandered into a saloon, the same location he found Tillie working. Jack followed them down the dusty streets. A tumbleweed rolled across the road, right behind the gang. The speed of his pacing increased. He knew his group would not be welcome in the inn. The foursome, unaware of segregation laws, spent too much time on the run.

The kids wandered down the street, past the hotel. They admired the burgeoning city with brick buildings, a vast storefront, and lavish and rundown hotels and saloons. They searched for a shop, hoping and praying their faces weren't plastered on storefront windows.

They noticed nothing; unaware a mysterious stranger had removed them the night before.

Jack strode into the bar. His crisp walk intimidated the patrons. Several customers stopped drinking to watch the man take off his black hat, set it in down on the bar, and order a straight shot of whiskey. He grasped a wad of cash from his money-clip.

"There's four kids, the oldest one used to ride with me, looking for a place to stay. He's with a couple of mixed-bred girls, and a little white girl. Give them a couple of rooms." Jack dropped a Jackson on the bar. "They'll be paying themselves. This is for you."

The bartender's eyes devoured the money, already spending it on anything. "Can't let no Injuns or niggers in here. Don't care what they mixed with. Your money ain't talking to me." He pushed it aside.

Jack reached under his jacket. He pulled out his revolver. "Well, if my money ain't speaking to you, maybe this will." He aimed it at the barkeep. The barrel pointed straight at his eyes. Jack cocked the weapon, his finger itchy on the trigger. Any second a bullet would be through his head, shattering a bottle of whiskey. A piano player played The Yellow Rose of Texas, boisterous men sang along with the ditty. Jack's finger tapped to the beat, but still on the trigger.

The bartender grabbed the currency. "Maybe your money speaks my language. I'll let those kids spend the one night. One night only."

"That's all they'll need. Some rest, some grub, and some bathing. No whores or whiskey needed. I'm sure they got their own whiskey. Now, tell that banjo picker and piano player to get loud. I'll be back in the morning. I need my whore." He tucked the gun back in its holster, adjusted the jacket over his belt. He turned and strolled down the street, past the tumbleweed, and back to the Mobberley. The sinister man smiled all the way.

Paul heard the collection of Stephen Foster songs from down the street. He spun around, drifting back towards the music. The others in the group drifted behind him.

Paul took charge. He paid for two rooms, one for the girls, one for himself, even though he wanted to share with Sara, or Kaydence, who may be more willing to be his for the night. He wanted the older Creole girl. They bunked down, the three girls across the hall from the songster. His guitar played throughout the night, recollecting their journey so far. It was nowhere here near half-way done.

The girls rested, while Paul wandered down the steps toward the saloon after a bath. The thoughts of the Indian or the Creole became overwhelming, but he'd cross forbidden boundaries. His job was to get the three to Tulsa, not to make one a young mother. There'd be whores in the saloon if he desired a tumble with a woman. He ambled downstairs into the saloon. A fancy dressed man in dark pants, white shirt with a bolo tie descending his chest, sat playing poker. The tie was highlighted with a turquoise jewel around his neck. Paul didn't recognize him. Jack seemed relieved. Dressing up, a shave and a haircut became the perfect disguise.

Paul wandered through the saloon, looking for action, checking for a whore who might satisfy his need for an hour, maybe longer. The women casing the saloon were heavier set than others, and older than what Paul craved. They ignored the boy, their eyes upon other drifters and rail workers.

Jack enjoyed the cards. He spun his head, an eye on the kid. Muffling his voice, he called out to his unassuming partner. "Kid, them women here are no good. We can deal you in a few hands. You look mighty tired. There are a few snorts of the whiskey here and some poker gonna do you in for the night, anyway."

Paul stared hard at the speaker, wondering if he'd seen that man before. Jack's eyes narrowed. The clean-cut professional Leroux's eyes were now wide, hypnotizing the young man towards the table. Paul strode over, bow legged from riding the horse for miles. He glanced around the table. The men were all dressed nice, and looked clean cut. Paul peered at the gentlemen, then at the empty chair that seemed to be reserved for him. Glancing at the man in the turquoise enhanced bolo tie, a small smile emerged, and quickly dissipated. He sat in the chair, accepted the glass of whiskey from the bottle they passed around.

"I don't have much money," Paul told them, "just some from selling some hides and such. I can only sit in for a couple of hands, unless I win a few." He snickered.

Staring straight ahead, no small talk allowed, the men were all professional poker players on the way from Dallas. They were all staying at the Mobberly, but refused the patronage from the wandering ladies of the evening for several rounds of blackjack. LeRoux shuffled and dealt from the bottom with the best of them. Paul won the first four hands. He kept playing, drinking, and winning a few hundred dollars from his former boss. The rest of the table became suspicious, and this wasn't luck for the kid, but some shady dealing going on. Two of the men, one wore a turquoise broach on his bolo as well, got itchy. Paul noticed he carried no weapon. The kid didn't search out gunfire, only rest and relaxation, maybe a whore, but he got roped into a card game with professionals. He was winning and realized why. He knew the dealer and assumed the table figured out the cheating. Paul brushed most of his winnings to the center of the table, not claiming them.

"Been riding the last week. I need some shut-eye." He stretched his legs and rose and grabbed a tiny handful of the winnings, enough for a washed-up whore, and strode over to one. He plopped the money into her hands, and she escorted him to her room, where they stayed an hour.

He left, wanting to head to his bed, but thought better of it. It was time to skedaddle while Jack LeRoux waited for them. He had set them up for something, and if LeRoux masterminded something, it would not be good. The girls never locked the door. He walked in and climbed into bed with Sara and Kaydence, causing them to wake up. Sara woke first. She wiped the crust out of her eyes. "It's not even one. Why you waking us?"

He didn't want to alarm her. Rose always feared Jack. "Come with me." He pointed towards the far end of the room.

Sara forced herself from the bed. She followed her friend. "He's here, Jack, and he's all clean shaven, and dressed slick. However, I noticed the tiny scar and I'm not sure if he knows. I think he's setting us up."

"Let's go to your room so we can discuss this in private," she whispered to him.

They crouched away from the two sleeping girls, slipped out, and snuck across the hallway. They tip-toed across the wooden floors of the cheap hotel room, listening to the loud sounds a whore made with one patron in the adjacent room.

The moans were loud and fake, but both tuned them out. "Okay, I'm awake." She noticed the glow in his eyes resembling the protective devil he'd become. "This is part of the plan. I had a vision. This is for Rose and her upbringing. She needs this,so we can't teach her to run, but to confront problems."

"Yes, but I rode with him for years, so I know what he can do. You saw him there in Logansport shooting them boys so there wouldn't be no witnesses. He had me kill the other member with a shot in the back."

"He ain't gonna do anything to us. I'm not sure you know who he is, or who you are? This is bigger than taking Rose to Tulsa. Something is going to happen in Tulsa, and we need to be there."

He leaned in, rolled his eyes, curiosity getting the best of him. "I don't know my pappy; I can tell you that. LeRoux picked me up at an orphanage in Tulsa when I was five and he never told me nothing about his past. I fled from him when I was eight, lived with some folks in Ft. Worth, some guy named Clarence. He was a cattle rassler, who stole from everyone. That's where Jack found me. He never explained nothing to me. I have been riding with him for the last two years, and he has been keeping me safe, away from danger, and shoots anybody who might threaten me. You know I've been trying to run away from him the last year, and I was relieved when he took off. I think he's doing something big; we don't want no part of."

"What he has planned will help us get Rose and you home. We might not like this, but we need to follow the plan. Do you think he knows you recognized him?"

"I'm not sure. He's always one step ahead of us."

"We need to play it like we don't."

"I might have messed up. We were playing cards, and I won every hand Jack dealt. The strangers at the table looked itchy, like we were conning them. I noticed their fingers getting itchy to do some shooting, so I got out, left the winnings on the table and left."

"I'm sure you did the right thing. You ain't supposed to get in a shootout at this place. Marshalls would be all over us, and Marshalls would haul me back to Louisiana to hang me."

"I'm confused," he whispered to her. Their eyes locked.

"I am too." She leaned towards him. He inched closer. "No, we can't, not until Rose and you get home."

"Is she my sister?"

"Nope, I'm figuring this out as we speak. She's the vessel to take you home."

Paul, still puzzled, glanced at the ceiling a few times. He shook his head, unsure of this conversation and wondering who this girl was. She intrigued him. Maybe she wasn't some young woman forced into a life on the run, but a woman owned by the devil. He never thought the devil consumed him. He got to his feet, walked across the room, and returned. The moaning next door ceased. "Okay, I don't understand none of this, but we'll stay."

"I don't understand none of it either, but follow my lead. Trust me, we'll make it to Tulsa. You and Rose will stay., Kaydence and I will turnaround, and get back to Louisiana." Sara stood and nudged the door open. She peaked out the door, noticed someone walking towards the stairwell and figured it was the customer. She crept across the hallway into their room. Kaydence laid in their bed sleeping. She crawled in beside her, wondering if her native sister knew she slipped out of the room.

Chapter 21

The man was well-dressed again in black pants, a white shirt, but with a different bolo tie, ornamented by a lone star signifying the great state the quartet passed through. He glanced at the youth, while they ate a breakfast of bacon, eggs and flapjacks. They sipped their coffee, oblivious to the well-groomed man stalking them. Jack lit a small cigar, stepped out of the hotel lobby, then strolled down the street to the Mobberly. There his horse rested, tied to a hitching post. He ascended the wooden spiral staircase, informed Tillie he would be unable to escort her anywhere in the next two days.

"I got business in Ft. Worth. After that, you and me will head to Monterrey."

He changed clothing. The proper attire dropped, replaced by a wardrobe that reflected his true character. He adorned black, black jeans, a shirt, topped by his black hat. Jack grimaced at the mirror, since he had missed the whiskers, but still looked professional. Taking his knife, he made a small incision on his cheek. He needed evil since he was still clean cut and hated it. The lone star on his bolo sat proudly under his chin. His three pistols were all loaded; the outlaw gallivanted out the door down to the lobby. Jack climbed into the saddle of his trusted steed, and they trotted down to the other hotel.

Sara took charge. She expected the worst, knowing they were required to be roped into Jack's plan. However, she knew what he had in store, or when he'd initiate it. Towards the depot which laid across the street, a passenger train sat. Many of the exiting passengers dressed like in the highest fashion and appeared wealthy. The train faced west, more than likely heading to Dallas and Ft. Worth. Those two cities had more wealth in them than Longview. Wealthier people flocked to money. Sara looked at Paul, her spiritual confidant, his eyes reflected. Kaydence and Rose roamed the streets, keeping in spotting distance of Paul and Sara.

Paul whistled to get Sara's attention. They eyed the lone man, dressed in black, topped with a black hat, trotting atop a pure black stallion. Sara stepped away from departing passengers. She moved to the side, straight into his path, hands on her pistol. If he didn't stop, she would make him, even though that wasn't part of the plan. But then again, it might have been.

The man pulled up on the reins. The horse lifted its front legs, slowed, and came to a complete stop. Jack dismounted. "You found me. I had other business that needed attending to."

"I know, your father told me." Sara's hands remained clutched on the pistols. Kaydence and Rose crossed the street towards the animals. Paul stood in the shadows, pistol in hand, in case needed. Sara watched him dismount. Dust formed as his feet plopped on the dirt street.

The other three strode towards them. Sara and Jack continued a stare down, neither flinching, though none was about to draw a weapon. They would be no standing back-to-back, counting ten paces, turning and firing, one dropping to their death, or maybe both. The trip to Tulsa was required more for Paul and Jack than for Rose. However, no one knew why. Rose needed her family.

Jack and Sara strolled down the dusty street, away from the others. Paul attempted to follow, but Jack spun around, lifted his hand to cease the youth in his tracks. Jack motioned him towards the horses and gear. Paul moseyed in that direction. He had ridden with Jack long enough to identify his hand movements, when to mosey, and when to skedaddle.

"We're here for a reason," Jack told her without hesitation. They were out of listening distance. "I owe an enormous debt; part of the debt was to get you out. You don't know your cousin, but he's an influential man in Ft. Worth. The people I've killed all worked for him, even the crew in Logansport. Well, some of them. I work for him as well, but will only deal with him. I owe him money, and we need that money to finish this journey. Otherwise..."

"The journey will cease, we will die." Sara finished his sentence.

"Exactly. I had to see the man before the rest of the journey. All three of you are required for this. Even the little kid. It's going to be dangerous; He may shoot us. Paul will protect the two other girls. You will be my partner. I hope you're ready to ride. Our first mission will be a training mission. Let's get go for a ride. We need to be in Ft. Worth in two days, plus we need a lot of money."

They spun around towards the other three. This time, their strides elongated as they had a purpose. Saddlebags packed, weapons in hand, all five rode off towards Dallas near a trail adjacent to the railroad tracks. They stopped for a meal break and resting the equine north of Tyler, where they camped out. They shot and ate critters along with jerky and berries. Jack relaxed and pulled his hat over his head. Rose fell asleep. Sara, Kaydence, and Paul sat by the fire.

Paul whipped his guitar out. "I love to play this thing by the fire. I think the flames accent the sound." He hummed a ditty, the words unintelligible, but the guitar sounded influenced by the flame, or someone or something else.

Kaydence watched through the flashing of the flames, and Sara noticed the infatuation in her eyes. She had to keep her friend's lust in check.

"Let's walk over here," she told Paul, pointing to a lone tree in the open so there would be no temptation. He rose and followed her. They watched Kaydence grab her bag. She strolled towards them and laid beside Sara. All three fell asleep and woke with the sun.

After a quick morning meal and basic morning duties, they mounted their horses and rode south towards the railroad track. Paul received Jack's instructions. The information was like the Indiana farm kids that Jack splattered on the tracks. Kaydence and Rose dismounted Kaydence armed, Rose observing and learning the proper way to rob a train.

Jack and Sara hung behind them. The train whistle blew. They noticed the steam ascending in the eastern sky. It was time. Jack trusted Paul; they had been down this route. Sara never robbed a train before, despite a mean streak in the girl. She knew she'd steal from the rich, there was a noble cause to   it.

Sara kept her field glasses on Paul. She gave him a silent signal, one she received from Jack. Paul rode out on his horse and stopped in the middle of the tracks. The sun cast a shadow behind Paul as the train slowed down. Paul struggled to control his horse, which was tempted to get off. Faces covered with bandanas like true outlaws, Kaydence soon joined him, revolver in hand as they boarded the stopped train.

Weapons pointed at the engineer; Kaydence spoke. "This is for stealing our land and moving us away." She cocked her pistol.

"We're robbing this."

Paul and Kaydence kept their guns pointed, and one false move from the railroad employees would be their last. Rose stayed in the shadows.

Sara and Jack boarded the train from the rear. They hopped over the railing into the first-class section, collecting cash and jewelry from the passengers. They strolled up through the aisles, guided by the plush chandelier lights that hung from the ceiling of the railcar. The leather seats were all occupied with older, silver-haired passengers, who were not afraid to relinquish their jewelry, however clinging to their money. Both Jack and Sara pointed their pistols at the passenger's brains. No one challenged them. They hopped to the next car, stealing what they could, and continued towards the front. They stole the mail, hopped off before the lowest class of the train, and signaled Rose to notify Paul and Kaydence to depart from the engine.

A railroad porter decided to be a hero. Jack LeRoux shot him dead, his limp body dangling on the steps of the lead passenger car. They fled, all five vanishing into the forest. They started east towards Longview, waiting for the engine to start again. The train sat stationary, with the porter's body swaying in the North Texas breeze.

In private, Jack told Sara. "He's one of them, a sacrificial lamb of an empire. They'll be coming after us. Damn Texas Rangers, I hate them. They're not part of the empire, but they don't know when to leave this crap alone. We wouldn't have to rob and kill to feed the empire if they let my man live his life."

Sara thought she understood. Her God was a guardian, and she needed to follow his will. Jack followed the same God. This God and Jack were both tricksters, however, this journey required faith. The five headed west; vanishing through the fields toward Dallas.

Deeper in the forest, they followed the railroad. The horses galloped, fleeing the crime scene. They sprinted twenty miles before requiring a break. The equine drank and ate berries. The outlaws grabbed a quick bite. Paul came to Sara.

"Jack is required to die tonight." His monotone sounded as if it came from another being. "One of us must do it. It might be me, you, Kaydence, or even Rose. We will receive guidance from Him. This is to save our lives and souls." He vanished deeper into the forest. Soon, his haunting guitar drowned out the sound of the rushing creek.

Jack rode up on his horse. "We need to roll."

Sara stared at him. Kaydence studied his movements. Rose sat beside a tree, seeming afraid of him. He finagled his horse through the thick woods, heard Paul's guitar sing a tune of death, and he stopped the horse. "Sara, get the boy out here."

Sara sat still, since it wasn't time for action. She stalled him, gathering her gear, keeping jewelry and cash for herself. She had to, if the man was to be murdered in self- defense that evening.

The guitar sang. Sara heard the calling. So did Rose. Kaydence strolled towards the gear and equine. The girl took on her roll, initiating the packing of the horses. She relished the role, taking pride in her efficiency. The campfire burnt out, the embers no longer burning, and it was past the time to ride. Rose stood behind Sara while Paul picked the last note of a new song he messed with. He set his hands on the ground, pushing himself to his feet. He flipped his music instrument on his back, stretched his arms vertically, twisting his head upwards to gleam at the sky, as if he talked to God. Sara lifted her head up too, while Rose followed her lead. Sara was her savior. At that moment, she discovered a new God or goddess. They set the plan.

Jack led the way west. Once they got to Ft. Worth, he would be home free. The four others would be on their own, set up to be captured. He was a trickster who made deals with different gods, guardians, and leaders of evil empires. The man, shifty, but was Clarence Bourgeois' right-hand man. If it wasn't for Jack LeRoux, Clarence Bourgeois would go by his original name, Cletus Barnum, and would be a fugitive.

The group rode hard again, since they hijacked the railroad, which is a federal offense. US Marshalls, Texas Rangers, including vigilante hunters, wanted them and reward posters would hang in store windows and on trees. The five had to be smart. They needed to ride fast, and they needed to stay in hiding.

Again, they settled down for the evening. The campfire kept low, not to be noticed by anyone in pursuit. They enjoyed a meal and some whiskey. Kaydence sat closer to Paul than Sara preferred. Jack eyed Sara, scowling at the young woman. He looked bored again, arose, paced around the fire, while keeping his eyes on Sara. Jack studied her face, body, and the movement of her legs. He watched the way she stretched them out, her boots touching the low burning fire. Rose saw him sneer at the oldest girl, the one past womanhood as he paced around the fire, never taking his eyes off her. He stood back across the circle of flames to get out of the smoke. He rested his head on his hand. Sara stretched her legs. The smile on Jack's face increased when Sara pulled her hat over her head, closing her eyes, hiding from the world.

Rose scooted closer to Sara like a cat protective of its owner. She stretched her arms above her head, opened her mouth with a giant yawn, and placed her head on Sara's stomach. A sleeping Sara put her hand on Rose's shoulder. Paul refused Kaydence's advance; however, Kaydence's head fell asleep on Paul's shoulder underneath the oak tree. Jack stood guard, making sure no bounties chased them. He as well monitored Sara, sneering as he watched her doze. Morning came, and the five stayed hidden in the woods until deciding it was time to ride. They rode hard and safe keeping would be in Ft. Worth. One night and one more day of riding would be required. At sundown, they arrived in Terrell, Texas. A man, dressed in a giant ten-gallon hat pulled down and shading his eyes, greeted Jack, while the other four followed. He looked over at Jack's crew.

Rose could stay, Paul he wondered about. Minorities were not allowed in town after dark, and Mr. Bourgeois doubted Paul. Even with his paler features, he looked like mixed. One look at Kaydence, and he knew she was an Indian. Sara, he smiled at, since they set the trap for her. The large man stood at the town's edge. He murmured to Jack LeRoux and turned his head at the others.

"Rose, c'mon up. Come meet the man who will get you to Tulsa. This is Clarence Bourgeois."

Terrell, Texas, the type of town scattered through the south, didn't allow minorities after sundown. Jack LeRoux knew this, though the rest remained clueless to this law and the town boundaries. This was Clarence's town; this was his territory. He knew Sara Barnum, and he knew her father, but he knew the mother. In fact, he aided her escape some thirty years earlier.

Sara knew when and where the trap would be set. She signaled Rose to ride to the side, away from the action. Sara expected the kid riding by her side. Signing with her hand, she continued communicating with the youngin, until Rose and her steed trotted towards the two older men. She stood a few yards away to the side, not wanting to be in the expectant crossfire. Rose kept her pistol hidden, however, her right hand descended to her tiny waist.

Paul and Kaydence eyed Jack and the large man. Their hands came off the reins, lowered to the revolvers on their belts. Jack was a bloodthirsty man with fast hands.

Sara and Rose gawked as Jack unloaded the stolen goods from the train robbery to the fat man. He didn't have them all. Sara carried the rest. Jack spun around on his horse.

"Hey, young lady. You got two choices right now," the fat man spoke out loud. His accent, a tint of Texan, but hinted from Louisiana. "The first is to bring me the loot." He glanced behind him. The sun still displayed on the horizon, but it sank fast, like a rock in the river. "No niggers in this town after sunset, so we got every right to shoot ya and your Injun friend."

The two retreated on their horses. Sara had to cross the town boundary, even though she did not know where it was.

Tumbleweeds dashed across the dusty streets, interrupting the showdown. Sara paid no attention to the plants somersaulting towards her. Her eyes remained on the targets. The men glanced away from her, starting a slight movement on her hands which clutched her revolver.

Oblivious to the happenings, a mule-driven cart crossed behind Paul and Kaydence. The native girl watched the wagon, a smile overcoming her in acknowledgement of an upcoming victory. Kaydence's mental focus remained on Sara, sending her Caddi Ayo's message, and hoping Sara received   it.

Sara's hands clenched the revolver tighter. Both men studied her moves. Jack's hands remained at his side in full display.

"So, where's the town line? I don't want to get shot crossing an imaginary line. Why don't you come and get the goods?"

The fat man bellowed; his belly shook like most jovial fat men do when they laugh hard. "Clarence Bourgeois ain't gonna doing what some kid tells him. I run this town, ya hear me? That little girl can cross." He turned his head. Sundown approached. Darkness drifted upon the little railroad community.

Sara glanced at Rose, then at Clarence, and peered directly at Jack's hands. She took a breath. "So, if I cross this line, where I don't know where it is, to give you the jewelry I stole for you, you're gonna shoot us all. And if I stay still, you'll probably shoot me as well."

Jack's hands became restless. Clarence reached for his pistol. "C'mon Sara, I'm the only family you got, besides my kids. They're scattered all over the place, and they be looking for ya. I'm the only one who will get that girl to Tulsa." Rose looked across at Sara. Kaydence and Paul stood in the shadows. None of them flinched. The sun vanished, only a glow of orange sat in the Western sky.

"What if I bring you the goods?" Paul asked.

"You'll be shot dead, too. You can't cross. I know your father as well." Clarence's hand clenched his pistol, freeing it from his holster. "Only the girl may proceed."

Rose, on cue, kicked her horse in the kidney, hard like Sara taught her. It charged at Jack and the fat man. Chaos ensued. Jack fumbled with his pistol; couldn't get a grip and it fell to the ground. Sara shot at Clarence. The girl could hit a squirrel at fifty yards. Nailing an obese man at twenty feet simple. She shot again for good measure. He plopped on the ground. Blood seeped through his white shirt. His face made an indention in the sand.

Jack LeRoux never got a chance to fire his weapon. Paul never got revenge on the older man he rode with. Kaydence sat on her horse, gawking. Rose, with a rifle in hand, the kick of the gun knocked her on her back. She looked at Sara. Sara didn't smile back, even though the kid saved her life. Kaydence remounted her horse. The four vanished into the North Texas forest.

Part III

Chapter 22

No one spoke. They rode hard until the horses couldn't go any further. Bounty hunters, Texas Rangers, US Marshalls, and vigilante Bourgeois roamed the woods. They wouldn't last long. They needed divine intervention. The four survivors sat in a circle, surrounding a small fire. Flames burned low. Hunters haunted the North Texas forest. Sara and the three younger ones sat crossed-legged, heads bowed, each praying to their gods. Sara and Paul's God got them this far and became a part of the plan.

The trickster might be unhappy with the death of one of his followers, especially at the hands and rifle of a Jesus follower and would not be trustworthy. He might not have been trustworthy, anyway. They were still alive, and this man worked in ways no one understood. He required feeding; however, the tobacco ran out, and the whiskey running low, and there was no way they could replenish it.

Rose wondered if her murdering a cold blood killer at eight years of age could be forgiven. She knew as a Christian Jesus would forgive her, if asked hard enough. She prayed, but watching a man fall off a horse, dripping in blood, she could never forget. The three girls heard her praying unintelligible words, pleading for guidance and forgiveness. Yet he offered no plan.

Kaydence stood up slowly. Her body rose from the ground, making her appear taller than normal. She peered over her group, taking charge of the situation. She waited until she garnered her group's attention. "I spoke with Caddi Ayo. Jack Leroux was of native blood. He wasn't Caddo, but of a neighboring tribe. We will be protected. However, those who did the sacrifice must bury him. We have tombs across the river for his body to rest. Once they bury him, we will be free."

The campfire burnt way down. Paul could not see across a few feet in front of him. "We have to steal his body, bury it in your mounds and talk to Caddi Ayo? How are we going to do that?" Paul's eyes glowed. Sara and Kaydence looked at each other, and twisted their heads away like a schoolboy who had the crush on the red-head girl in arithmetic class.

Kaydence rose as her tired legs struggled, but her youth took over. The crew listened to the Indian girl pace around the fire. All three looked at her face through the flickering light until her pacing ceased. "We don't. Someone has been following us all along, giving us protection. Do you remember the wagon? My people have been watching us. That man was a traitor to our people. He wanted us to leave Louisiana. He was supposed to die, and now he is a sacrifice to Caddi Ayo. My people are out there. We need to find them. They should have the body. I will ride off tonight searching. You three do not move until I return." Kaydence mounted her horse, aware Caddi Ayo had the answers. She would not argue with her friends. Riding into the darkness, she trotted alone, determined to find her renegade tribe. Her friends never thought she might be the sacrifice, maybe a diversion to draw attention from the vigilantes. Paul, Sara, and Rose watched her shadow meander through the dark forest, then huddled over the low fire, waiting for her return.

Rose lay next to Sara, curled up in her arms. Paul scooted over towards Sara. "We need to follow her," Paul said. "She's on her own. I don't remember a wagon."

Sara, her head in her hand, flipped her hat off and swished her hair. She stood up, similar to Kaydence earlier. The spirit took over. "I remember a wagon coming in right after he fell. The person driving the wagon looked faceless. However, darkness came. I didn't get a look at him. We need to stay. She'll return tonight."

"This is hard for me to understand," Paul retorted, setting the guitar next to an oak. He stretched his body. "I'm not sure if I even follow any of this. No one ever told me my purpose, at least I haven't figured it out. Just help me out." Once again, his eyes flashed in the dark.

"Does he even know his true identity?" Sara wondered to herself.

"You'll get it. Your destiny is to get me to Tulsa." Rose's voice came out of nowhere.

Sara's voice seemed to come from the sky, resonating deeper- Godlike. It circled the trio. "This trip has worn us out. We are all discouraged and need to lift each other up. Rose has tasted blood, and no one expected that. You and me, we've seen it most of our lives, and are tired of it. We need to speak to that man again, ask him to break free of any agreement. We've been on the run for too many nights. Kaydence is coming back, so things will be fine."

"We can sleep in the wagon, can't we?" Rose asked. "I'm getting tired, but my body doesn't want to sleep."

Sara exhaled, almost extinguishing the fire. She bowed her head. "Of course."

Rose plopped her head on Sara's saddle bag. She lay on her side with her face away from the other two. Paul moved back next to Sara and placed his arm around her, nudging her close. "I'm sorry, I should lead us."

She brushed his hand away, wanting it, but not wanting his closeness. "I need to feel the spirits from Caddi Ayo. Your touch isn't helping." She witnessed a softness in his eyes. Guilt ripped through her, but she needed a private time.

The night sky, silent, the sounds of wild animals howling, and wind shuffling the leaves of the trees, but there was nothing unusual. No sounds of bounty hunters. They were used to people following them. Her head shot up. She glanced at Paul, while realizing. Her noggin lowered again.

"My purpose is to take the girl to Tulsa, but why? Kaydence, my traveling companion, but she was called back. Her purpose was to sacrifice Jack LeRoux. He was an Indian as well, maybe not Caddo, but a brotherhood tribe. I'm not sure anyone knew until Kaydence did her part. This boy next to me is not really a gunslinger. There's a reason..." She stopped her thought. He pulled his hat down, so it covered his eyes. She glanced at the sky, then at the fire from which sparks no longer burned. The air had turned colder. "He didn't acknowledge me. He's hinted at being the trickster. The whiskey, the tobacco from earlier. Is he aware of his identity? Let me talk to him again through thoughts." Sara retreated from his presence. She found a tree to rest against and placed the back of her head against a pecan tree. She fell asleep, her hat over her eyes. Figuring this out became impossible. She survived so far on instinct.

She jumped from a vision. "They're coming, the bounties are after us. We need to skedaddle."

Rose and Paul stumbled to their feet, wiping their eyes, arms stretching above their head. The other two yawned. The sun had not crossed the eastern horizon, but it was already getting light.

"What are we going to do?" Paul asked. "We gotta ride. We're loaded with bullets and shells. Might have to take a few out, so be ready." They checked the guns, ammo, made sure they were packing and accessible. "They're surrounding us. Best we ride like the wind out of here towards the North."

Paul raised his hand. "That's what they be expecting." A hint of Louisiana Creole came through on his annunciation. "Bourgeois are everywhere between here and the border. I know a way, and you must trust me. You've depended on me so far. Follow me." Guitar on his back, rifle in hand, he mounted his horse. Rose, armed with a rifle, as well took off behind Paul. Sara debated splitting up, and then she saw Paul and Rose vanish through the forest. Kicking the horse with her boots, she tugged the rein and let it gallop, following the trail. Sprinting through the open fields, the three headed north. No bounty hunters were present. Sara caught up with the two in a few miles, and they pushed the equine harder. It was time for a break when they approached a small stream. They had ridden for about fifteen miles. Paul and Rose dismounted as Sara rode in. She plopped off her steed, still trying to catch her breath, led it to lap up some water. Rose gathered berries and sought critters out for a bite to eat. Paul built a fire, sat while the embers burned down. Sara watched them both.

Rose glanced at Sara. "They're not coming now." Her voice was in a monotone, and her speech was slow, and it reminded Sara of death. "Paul wrote a new song, protecting us. I heard it on the way up as we rode."

Sara glared at her. Paul sat against a lone tree, guitar in playing position. Sara strode up to him, each stride longer, hands on her hips. "Rose said you got a new song. I want to hear it."

"I ain't got no time to write a new song. I gotta get us out of here. Look, ain't no bounty hunters here." He kicked back, relaxed, letting mystic powers take control. His hands struck the guitar, strumming. He played a series of chords, leading with a G.

Rose hummed. "We need to roll along, Sara. After we get a bite to eat and rest up."

These days are gone, only you and me moving on."

Paul kept strumming and then sang.

My days are done now,

Take this girl home
I've got her this far now
Take her to the Cimarron
Indian Nations waiting
bring this girl home.
I'm revealing everything
Take her to the Cimarron
Devil took a hold, and devil took control of me
Bounties need to follow, so you may roam free
They may chase me down, but you must roll along
To the river they call Cimarron
We must say goodbye
You are on your own
And no time to cry
Take her to the Cimarron.

Rose and Paul sang harmonies, even though Paul played from his head. This was the song Rose sang, the one Paul wrote for her. They alternated verses, Paul leading.

Sara peered into his eyes. Paul glanced down at hers. "This was the only way. I've been with you the entire time." His complexion darkened. He aged right before her. His features returned to the young white man. He grabbed a corncob pipe out of his pocket and lifted a pouch of tobacco. He took a small pinch, placed it in the pipe's bowl. The man searched his pockets for a flask. Sara watched him dig through his saddlebag.

She strolled towards her gear. He watched her and smiled. She pulled out a flask, walked over to him, handing it to the devil. "Keep it, I don't need it now, but I might need a snort for the road." She took a drink and then another swallow. Shaking her head, she looked up at Paul. He appeared to be the gangly white kid again.

They continued peering into each other's eyes. She presented the flask to him.

He took a couple of swallows, smiled, and lit the pipe in the stiff breeze. "They will follow me but won't capture me. They can't trap me." He leaned down to kiss her. The kiss lasted a few seconds, long enough for Sara to miss him. When she opened her eyes, Paul was gone and Sara heard the hooves pounding the dirt. There was over one set grinding against the soil.

"We're on our own now. This is going to be the easiest part of the journey, though the longest, I don't even think we are half-way there. I'm still not sure if we can catch a train or not. I'm still wanted, and just like me, you are, too." She looked at her young friend, who was busy gathering up her saddle bag.

"Well, just like me, you're an orphan as well." She looked up at Sara, who had become a mother figure to Rose, afraid to leave her. The two of them on horseback trotted towards Oklahoma through the North Texas prairie. At last, they rode in peace, wondering how long that would last.

Chapter 23

The ride north was uneventful. They approached the Red River dividing Texas from Indian territory, and Sara wondered about Kaydence, hoping she would see her Caddo friend again. She thought about her family; the ones forced to walk from Louisiana to Central Oklahoma, and how many perished along the way. They rode up to a bluff overlooking the Red River. The two of them searched for a ferry with men pulling a log raft. She remembered shooting the men along the Sabine River. Two men who might have killed or raped her. Her second and third killings. Her and Rose sat astride their horses, glancing around the river valley. Sara bowed her head to pray aloud, so Rose could witness her confession.

"Please, forgive me for the blood that was shed on this journey. You gave me a journey, a mission to get this girl to her extended family. I'm not sure why you chose me, but maybe it was because I'm an orphan, and circumstances made this child one too. Again, forgive me for the blood that was shed, and please protect us while crossing the river, as we head through the Nations. In Jesus' name, amen."

"Amen," Rose retorted, head bowed in her own brief prayer. "Thank you for Sara, who has protected me on this trip. I want to see my uncle, his family and, of course, the Newcombs. Make sure you keep Sara safe. I look up to her like she's my mother. If it wasn't for her, I'm not sure what would have happened. In Jesus' name, amen." She glanced at her mentor and smiled. They spotted the ferry operators descending the bluff. Meandering through a thicket of pecan trees, the two came to the river's edge. On the other side sat the ferry operators.

"We ain't got no money," Sara called out to them. "We got a couple of racoon furs we can trade for some ferrying." The furs were worth more than a haul across the river. Sara felt it was a fair trade at this point. Once inside Indian Nations, they'd be free.

Beside their steeds, they watched the men pull the raft across the river. As they got closer, Rose scooched closer to her mentor, pulling Sara's arm. Sara glanced down and saw Rose shaking.

"What's wrong?" Sara glanced up.

The two men grinned, both armed with pistols, their faces familiar. Both darker complected and a little chubby reminded Rose of the fat man Sara shot in Terrell.

"Bourgeois," Sara said loud enough for Rose to hear. "We'll do what we have to," Sara whispered into her younger friend's ear.

"I'm ready for this life." Rose smiled; her gaze fixed into Sara's eyes.

"I'm tired of it, but…"

The younger of the two men, who seemed to be brothers, stepped off the ferry. Missing a couple of teeth, whiskers descending his face, he eyed both girls. Sara and Rose boarded the ferry. The younger brother pulled the raft across, tugging on a thick rope. He grunted and tugged, then stopped pulling as the raft came to a rest halfway across the flowing water.

"Jeb, we got the girl who killed Uncle Clarence. We knew she be headed this way." He reached for his pistol but failed to grasp it.

Sara was quick on the draw. One Bourgeois lay dead, and his younger brother soon followed, with Rose following Sara's cue. They both blew the smoke away from the revolver and smiled at each other.

"What should we do with them?" The wide-eyed eight-year-old asked her tutor.

"What do you want to do with them?"

"Kick them in the river, feed some fish maybe." Rose glanced at the dead men.

Sara peered at the bodies. "I'm thinking these guys need a boat ride. We'll send them cruising down the river." They tugged the boat to the Sooner side of the Red River.

Huffing and puffing, Rose smiled. "Why can't we do both?" She kicked the bodies towards the edge of the boat. Both corpses hung off the edge and with one good bump, they could fall off. Sara took her knife, slicing down through the rope, and they pushed it into the current and watched the raft drift. The bodies bounced on the raft. Sara handed Rose her field glasses, and they witnessed one brother plop into the river, while the other had not fallen by the time the raft vanished from view.

On the Oklahoma side, they asked Jesus for forgiveness again.

The horses trotted along in no hurry at the moment. No longer in Texas, or the United States, they rode up through the Indian Territories. Sara and Rose felt safe at last. Tulsa, still a week away by horseback, but they had ridden hard most of the trip.

"We're riding through Choctaw territory. Kaydence said they are a peaceful bunch. However, some elders felt a mistrust. I do speak Caddo; I'm hoping it won't hurt us. Let's mosey through here. We can bunk out, get some grub, and wander north."

"Aren't most Indians savages?" Rose kept her tiny hands on the reins, letting the horse trot up the bluff. The thick pine trees lined the cart part they followed. The trail dug deep with wagon wheels, letting them witness the prints of horseshoes along the way.

"Just like everyone else, I'm sure there are some we don't want to run into. But then again, Kaydence was a Caddo, and my Mama was black, while Daddy was white. Paul, I don't know, and Jack was a savage, but I think he was half Injun. I think you're all white, but I saw you shoot Jack. You can be savage if you want." She smiled at the girl. "Remember, we stayed with Kaydence's family. They were Indians and kind, loving and supportive. Let's get over this little ridge here and scout about. Kaydence mentioned The Choctaw are a friendly tribe. They have a brotherhood, sharing a language. We might stay a few days."

"I just want to see my uncle. Can't we take a train?" Her voice turned crass. She lowered her head, not taking in the scenic ride.

"Well, you know why we can't take the train. I still got goods we stole, and I'm hanging on to them. I'll sell or trade them somewhere. There are some Indians who don't like the railroad coming through, anyway. They'd want to trade stuff we stole from people. Look up here, we're getting to the top. Ain't this pretty?"

Rose glanced up. They had reached the apex of the bluff. Down in the valley, through the field glasses, Sara spotted a village and then spun around to look at where they came from. She could see the river in the distance, however, could not make out the ferry. She wondered about the other brother, if he still laid on the raft, or became bait for bottom feeders in the Red River. Her smile, sinister, the tips of her lips curled up. She took off her hat, swished her hair and wiped her brow. She presented Rose with the glasses.

"It is pretty up here." She stretched her legs, walking around, leading her horse along the way. "I wish we could stay up here." "You want to get to Tulsa, now you want to stay here," Sara smirked. "Which one?"

"Let's ride. Can you help me on? I'm pretty tired. We can rest once we get down to the village." Rose placed her foot in the stirrup, Sara gave her the required boost as the younger girl straddled her pony. Sara settled in the saddle. The grin returned to her face as they trotted down the trail. Sara got on her horse, admiring her charms, and soon took the lead to descend the trail.

Going downhill across the trail became easier for the equine. The two girls rode faster, not speaking. Halfway down, they took a slight break. Sara broke out her glasses and peered through them. She noticed a cart, a girl a little younger than herself, with men surrounding her, lifting a body out of the cart.

"Rose, come look. Remember Kaydence said folks rode through that town in Texas with a wagon? Did you see it?" She tried to focus more on the wagon and the girl.

"I don't remember at all. Why?"

"Let's ride up. I think I see Kaydence, and they might have Jack's corpse. We've been following them." She walloped her horse on the side. The mare picked up her stride, galloping down the hill. Rose's beast watched the other horse, and then followed its lead, galloping after Papa.

Chapter 24

T he Caddo girl spoke to an elder in her native language. "This man is yours. He's not Caddo." She waited for another elder to translate and then continued.

"He needs a proper Choctaw burial. We brought him here."

The Choctaw walked over to examine the body. "Someone killed him for sacrifice. Caddo likes to sacrifice their people. I hope this was not a mistake. Our people, if presented to our gods, can live again." He glared at Kaydence. "Any idea who shot this man?"

Kaydence looked straight at the man. She spoke English this time. "I was there. We rode with him, and he set us up. It was self-defense."

The man, dressed in a blue shirt adorned with a turquoise bola tie, his black hat protecting his scalp from the searing sun, sat atop his long, straight black hair. He paced around the body. Kaydence kept her focus on him. "You know who shot him then?"

Kaydence took a deep breath, not for once taking her eyes off the Choctaw elder. She spoke in Caddo. "Yes, it was a girl riding with us. She's a little kid, younger than me." Kaydence glanced over at the village, looking for a girl of a similar age to Rose. She spotted one and pointed her out to the Elder.

"Sir," she spoke again in English. "He was going to kill my friend and me. Neither of us are Choctaw. He worked with the white man and the devil. He was evil. Our other friend shot him to save our lives." She exhaled.

"Do you know where this girl is?"

"Not right now. They carried him off, so we may sacrifice the body. I thought he was Caddo. We sought protection for our journey." Kaydence glanced around and noticed riders in the distance sprinting down a hill. The elder followed Kaydence's eyes.

"Maybe that is them. They are on the same path you took in here."

"What will happen to them?"

He looked at the bullet hole. "This man is Choctaw; he will always be Choctaw. White man been killing us for no reason, however Caddo speaks the truth, so I believe you. Our relationship with them is good. You are our brothers and sisters. This man looks cursed with the white man's devil. He's half-breed, half-Choctaw, a white man and devil's blood in him. We will speak to the girl when we see her." He glanced back up the bluff, where the two girls descended.

"Looks like they will be here soon."

More men arrived, followed by the other villagers. Kaydence stepped back to watch them transport the body towards the tree line. They hoisted Jack LeRoux's corpse and carried the decomposing flesh to the edge of their village, next to the thick forest. Jack's corpse lay in the sun, waiting for the rays of the sun to decompose the body. Others in the village came to witness, in hope one of their brothers would come back to life.

The land flattened out as Sara and Rose descended the bluff. No longer needing field glasses to witness the Indian activities, Sara stalled her horse beside Rose's. The faces of the natives were still not recognizable, both gals realized the natives noticed them.

The ladies rode up another quarter mile. Women strolled around, washed clothes, in the middle of preparing the day's meal. Teens batted a ball with sticks and raced around a vacant lot. Sara put on her field glasses to observe the events, unaware of what the customs were.

"Look, it's Kaydence." She moved the glasses around. "I hope she's not in trouble. We need to ride down and check what is happening."

The girl dismounted her horse, sat on the ground, and burst into tears. "Sara, I'm scared. What if that guy I killed was one of them? They might try to get me."

"Kaydence is there, and I will let nothing happen to you. We're halfway there and still riding, aren't we? Let me talk to them." She dismounted, gave the lass a hug, and aided her back on the horse. "We're going to do this." They trotted down the trail, riding all the way into the village.

Small huts adorned the village as families scooted back and forth, while others watched the ritual of Jack LeRoux. Sara and Rose rode to the Elder, tall, raised hand halting the girls. Kaydence joined him.

He motioned the girls to get off their horses. As soon as Sara and Rose complied, he maneuvered his hand, giving the motion for them to follow him to the tree, where Choctaw men hoisted Jack Leroux's body towards the sky. The girls received a jarring view of the corpse. The Elder looked at Rose, realizing she's the one who pulled the trigger. "Can you tell me what happened to this man? He's one of us. White man been butchering us for way too long. We are a peaceful nation and are unhappy a warrior was shot dead by the gun of a white woman."

"May I speak for her? She's only a kid." The native glared at Sara, eyed Rose, and his look softened upon realizing the age of the girl. The sight of the short girl in braided blonde hair made him acknowledge that Kaydence's words might have been the truth.

"I will tell you what happened." Sara began. "This man was supposed to help us up to Tulasi." She caught her breath, looking into the man's eyes.

"He betrayed us and would have killed us. They set my Caddo sister and I up to be murdered. He was going to kidnap this girl." She glanced at the Choctaw Nation. They waited, anticipating a name. Sara studied the onlookers and then continued. "He partnered with my second cousin; a man named Clarence Bourgeois." She glanced again at the spectators, eager with anticipation.

No one acknowledged the name. She peered back at the Elder. He nodded in affirmation.

"Come," he said in English. "This man has haunted us for years." He walked while the girls followed on horseback. They entered a hut. "This man has the devil's blood in him. He teamed up with a man in Louisiana and Clarence Bourgeois to raise havoc amongst our people. Us Choctaw, we like to live in peace, farm, hunt, much like the Caddo."

"I have Caddo blood," Sara spoke in the language she learned growing up with Kaydence. "The girl there is my sister." She showed him the scar on her palm, where they exchanged blood. Kaydence raised her hand as well. The man noticed the scar and smiled. "You two are blood sisters, I see. What is your relation to the white girl?"

Sara glanced at Rose, then back at the Elder. "They butchered her parents and siblings in Louisiana. I took it upon myself to get her to her kin near Tulasi. Kaydence was chosen to come with me. That is where we met Mr. LeRoux, the deceased. He was to be our protection. I don't think I needed it." Her stoic expression turned into a smirk.

"The belief in too many gods can cause evil. This man, Jack LeRoux, has dealt with our gods, and a certain man you might know. It forced him to have a split tongue and divided allegiances. He is Choctaw. He needs a proper burial, so when he enters the next life, he will be pure. We leave him in the sun, his soul will return to the God of Sun. You three are welcome to stay here and ride in Choctaw territory. We will escort you through our nation and give you supplies and ride in a wagon. We are a peaceful nation. However, this man caused us wars with Caddo and the Cherokee, as well as the white man. He plays many sides. It's a sin against all religions to believe in more than one God. You must pray to one and one only. Whether it is the white man's religion, or the Caddo, or the Choctaw. Even if you believe in the trickster." He stared Sara straight in her eyes.

Sara didn't blink.

They spent the night and the next day. Kaydence aided in the deer's cleaning. Rose observed, absorbing the tribe's rituals. Sara wanted to ride off and go home, even though her home was with the Caddo, or in the swamps near the Coushatta. Yet there was no home for her. Her life would be an outlaw, and she evolved into a good one. She sat in the small mud-based hut, all three could stay in. Maybe she'd stay in Tulsa with Rose. She wanted to pray about it. She no longer knew her God. "Did I pray to too many gods?" She stared at the sky for answers. She peered towards the southeast, where Paul had left the group. "You were him all along. I don't know if I should thank you or not."

Children played on the reservation, running up and down. Women cooked, knotted, made pottery. Man hunted, led in prayers and conducted councils. Kaydence and Rose assisted the women. Sara remained alone in her hut. A tear descending her cheek. She kicked off her boots, disrobed and laid naked in the hut, wearing only her hat that covered her face.

She awoke in the same position, staggered out the door of the hut. Kaydence and Rose were nowhere inside their little house. She grabbed her clothes, since she needed to bathe and soak her clothes on the running creek nearby. She hadn't bathed since they left the Longview hotel. That was a week and four dead bodies ago.

She ran into a woman whose naked body was getting bronzed from the searing sun. A group of dark-skinned women, it was possible they assimilated with Creoles from Southeast Louisiana, smiled at Sara. She spoke Muskogean, the language of the Choctaw. The women led Sara to where they washed their clothes. They sat in the flowing stream, taking their bath and rinsing off the animal skin clothing Sara wore. The cool water from the mountains to the east cascading down their body felt refreshing. Sara gathered her clothes, continued her walk, shaking herself dry, while her companion did the same. The woman led her to her hut and handed her a beautiful dress, but not flattering. The ceremonial dress came down to her feet and scraped the mud as she walked and peered over the reservation. Kaydence and Rose each wore a similar dress, as Sara spotted them leaving a mud hut.

They hung out with the Choctaws for a week, adapting to customs that needed little change, since they were like the Caddo. They made more clothes, caught and hunted their food, lived with the Indians for about a week. The girls and the horses took advantage of the week's rest, but soon it was time to go. Choctaw land covered most of the Southeastern portion of the Nations, in current day Oklahoma. The girls soon received their escort through the mountainous region, arriving at the Northern boundary of the Choctaw territory. They reached the Arkansas river.

"This is the end of our nation right here," the elder informed the girls. "You stay on the South side of this and ride up. You'll be in Muscogee territory and follow the river up. If you are tired, we can stay here for the evening. The place you are going is peaceful. They are a civilized tribe as well. You speak the language. You will be fine. It should only be two days of riding, again follow the river to where it meets the other great river. We will feast tonight, and tomorrow morning you will head out into our brother's nation."

Sara felt confident about the trip. Eager to get an early start, she awoke before the rest, cooked breakfast on the open fire, and fired up some wild onions and eggs. The other three, noticing the fragrance, all walked over to where Sara stirred the mixture, grabbing utensils to scarf down the meal.

"You cook like us," the elder said. You are welcome on our land anytime." He presented the girls with more food for the remainder of the journey.

He straddled his horse and bid the girls a sad farewell, before riding off into the sunrise. The girls followed the river northwest. Rose received correspondence that her uncle lived just west of the confluence of the Cimarron River that flowed into the Arkansas. They started the last leg of the journey. Only sixty miles to go.

Chapter 25

The Arkansas river meandered through the Muscogee territory. Taking several breaks, Sara, Kaydence and Roses fished in the river, swam and rested. Even with the break in the Choctaw Nation, they remained fatigued. The expedition exhausted the girls. They hoped the murders, train robberies, ended. It was behind them. Then again, there was always something about the outlaw life that will forever exhilarate a person.

Tulsa, Oklahoma in 1888, was not a boom town yet. Oil had not been discovered. Black Wall Street had yet to be created, and no one predicted the massacre in The Greenwood district. The city hadn't been settled when Rose and Sara trekked through on horseback. The original name, Tulasi, was settled by residents of the five nations, and the term meant old town. Outlaw gangs settled in and around Tulasi because they were free from the US Marshalls. Last they heard; Rose's uncle farmed in an area about ten miles to the West of the burgeoning city.

At last arriving in the town of about two hundred people, they searched for Rose's uncle, who said he'd meet them here. His homestead sat a few miles west. Sara and Kaydence had intended on arrival, to rest a few days and turnaround, then Sara would venture back home to Louisiana. They expected an easy final day that entailed getting a hotel, meeting Rose's uncle, bidding the young blonde girl adieu, and riding the country back home.

The girls trotted into the burgeoning city, and past hotels, saloons, and tumbleweed plopping across the dusty street. Not a soul in sight except for the bouncing bushes. The new arrivals spread out like the outlaws they became, controlling the dust streets, searching the town, and getting a feel of the village.

Sara turned at a corner around the block and came to a stop in front of a church, and across the street was a saloon, a store sitting right next to it, and adjacent to the store sat a boarding house.

"Woah." She yanked the reins. Peering through the billowing dust on the dirt street, she hollered. "Company's coming. Let's get rolling."

A man, about twenty, staggered out of a saloon. His moustache was thick, his clothes in rags. Following him, another man of a similar age surveyed the streets. His gaze found Sara, who was closest to the saloon. Sensing the tension, Rose and Kaydence rode up to Sara.

Rose's uncle smiled. "Bittercreek, my niece is here. Rose, over here." He raised his pistol, beckoning her with his hand. His scratchy voice, ruined by too much whiskey and tobacco, struggled to cut through the blowing dirt. She didn't look up, tugging the reins and urging the horse to shoot forward. He hollered again. "Over here, Rose." His smile lit the way. He ran to her but tripped over stones that littered the dirt. It might have been the whiskey. She and her horse trotted towards her uncle and his companion. Both men brandished guns and hooted, while Rose galloped towards them.

Sara and Kaydence followed them from the crossroads of the dusty streets. The girls plopped their legs over their steeds, feet first, into the dirt. They strolled the beasts over to the corner and knotted the horses to the wooden hitching post. Rose became responsible for the introductions after she gave her drunk uncle a hug.

"Uncle Bill," she said. "This is Sara and Kaydence. They escorted me here." Uncle Bill tipped his hat to the girls.

"I appreciate what you fine ladies done for her. I got the telegram. Can't believe my preacher brother got slaughtered back in Louisiana." Sara attempted a curtsy. She knelt, but not that far down. "The ride was hell, but we made it. We must have had divine intervention." She peered around the corner, thought she noticed Paul for a second, then shook her head.

"I really appreciate it," Uncle Bill told Sara. "I'll take her back in the morning. Looks like the girl can ride. We'll crash out here for the night, anyway. Her Auntie don't enjoy seeing me and Bittercreek this way."

Bittercreek smiled, even though he was drunker than Bill. He took off his black cowboy hat, tipped and let it drop in the dirt. It blew a few feet away. He stumbled and chased after it, only retrieving it after it scooted away one more time.

He staggered back to his feet. "I'm going in for one more round, Bill. Tell that pretty little niece of yours, we all gonna meet in the morning. We can have some grub at one of these fancy dining halls and get packing." He stumbled back into the saloon. Two men aided him in the tavern. No one got a decent glimpse of the two assistants.

Rose and her uncle walked towards the hotel, with Kaydence and Sara following close behind. They stayed within   earshot.
Rose spoke to her uncle. "Sara taught me how to ride. Papa never taught me how to ride a horse before."

Bill shook his head. "That lil brother of mine couldn't do too much. Good man, good with numbers and a hard worker, but he'd rather do the books than work the land. That's why we were going to hire him. Fudge some of these books on the ranch for a bit." Her uncle attempted to put his arm around his niece. He missed, stumbled, and caught himself.

"She taught me how to shoot a pistol and rifle. I got mighty handy with this." She whipped out the revolver, spun it around on her finger, and placed it back in the holster.

In his drunken southern best, her uncle replied, "Well, we gonna need someone with an excellent shot around here. Lots of outlaws running around." Bill smiled, wondering if he said too much.

"The best outlaw trained her to roll through Texas, but I'm not the one who shot Jack LeRoux down." Sara spoke behind them. Rose and her uncle turned towards her. That lil girl could take credit for his hide. Sara smiled as they closed in on the boarding house.

Her uncle smiled at both. "Uncle Bill?"

"Yes Rose." He responded. The man glowed through his drunken stupor. They all stopped walking and stood in a circle, waiting for Rose's confession. "I'm the one that shot Jack LeRoux down. We've been on the run since." Her uncle scratched his thick moustache, pondered over the three girls, wondering if they knew everything. "You say Jack LeRoux's dead?" He continued fingering his whiskers.

Kaydence spoke up. "Yes, we saw him go down, then his body was taken to the Choctaw since he was a half-breed. His body was elevated, so his soul moves faster to the sky."

The scratching continued. Sara sighed, peering over the section of Tulsa. She dealt with Legba this entire trip; she knew the power of the Gods. Something wasn't right.

Refusing to walk into the tavern, Bittercreek entered. They strolled to a café to get some grub. Rose's uncle bought them some steaks that the girls scarfed down. They downed their root beer while he nursed a beer. Across the street, he rented a room into which the girls retired.

Two small beds occupied the room. Kaydence and Rose controlled each bed. Sara grabbed a blanket off of one, plopped the covering atop the floor, stripped naked and sat in the washbasin to remove the journey from her flesh. Drying off with a towel, she grabbed her clothes, folded them up to create a pillow and laid down without shutting her eyes. They had arrived in Tulsa; it wasn't time to turn around. Not yet.

The soft breaths of two girls' snoring amplified all over the room. The breaths awoke Sara to find the room lit with a lamp turned down. She gathered some clothing without paying attention to what she wore. Dressed in a shorter Choctaw dress that approached her ankles, with nothing underneath, she departed the room barefoot and straight into the Tulsa night. She glanced around the deserted streets for signs of life, or the afterlife. On the corner, she noticed him in the shadows wearing a cowboy hat. She witnessed an aroma as a pipe illuminated in the shadows.

Paul was there. Jack Leroux must be around. The shadow turned his head, flashed a guitar and said, "You made it to Tulsa, I see. Your journey is incomplete. I wrote you a new song." He picked a few chords. The hypnotic song worked as an aphrodisiac for Sara. She floated across the dark, dusty streets towards Paul.

He stopped playing, instead setting the guitar against a wooden post. She stood next to the kid and tried to make out his features. His complexion had darkened a bit. An older man arrived, who resembled the man she once helped make the whiskey for. He lit the pipe, letting the Louisiana perique tobacco fragrance the Oklahoma sky. Paul vanished into the gas lantern lit streets of the village. He disappeared as if the devil took hold of him. A familiar man reappeared, and he sneered, squinting eyes, which glowed red. Sara stared him down, not showing fear.

"We will steal you away from your friends. I think you're old enough." The devil continued the sneer.

"We?" Sara attempted a response.

"Yes, this got confusing when the little girl shot my partner. He wasn't supposed to die. Not yet. You didn't follow the plan." Sara Barnum glanced up at the full moon before attempting eye contact with the man. She sought other intervention, but the power the men held over her haunted her. "You and me, we need to go far away, some place your friends will never find us." He caught her arm in his fist.

"Come with me" He tugged her, pulling her forward. Sara squelched a squeal.

"I'm not going with you." She raised her voice, attempting to break free. It was no use.

"If Jack wasn't murdered, this could have come easy for the both of us. This is where this journey all went wrong." He dragged her towards an empty saloon save but one man. The transformed cowboy-turned-devil tossed her to the scar-faced, mustached man sitting alone at a table in the tavern. The man at the bar smiled. He sneered at Sara, repeating Paul's words. "This is where it got confusing and went wrong." He removed his hat, running both hands through his bushy hair. "Let's get out of these shadows. I have a room upstairs, much lighter where I can see you."

Sara never felt a shove, but stumbled forward. Jack Leroux grabbed her wrist. She felt herself being led towards his hotel room.

Sara tried to put up a lame protest, however she fought divine powers. Pushed onto the bed, she turned around quickly to look at Jack LeRoux, eyes wide and aware of what they expected of her. She thought about the Paul she knew serenading her under a cypress tree, in the east Texas bayou, the gangly youth with stringy hair who sang such magic. She liked that Paul, not the man he transformed into, and she hated Jack Leroux. So hard to imagine they were one in the same.

Paul's singing echoed throughout the room. "This is a love song for you, since we're all alone together". His voice intoxicated Sara. He sang about the endless roads, the burning campfires, and the entire trip. Jack ripped her dress off, which wasn't difficult with Paul's singing. Sara pushed back on the bed; Jack Leroux watched her stretch. A smile turned to a sneer as his pants dropped. The click of the pistol halted the transmigrated being from raping the young woman. Paul's focus remained on his mentor; the colt aimed.

"This is the reason we're in Tulasi?" Paul's pistol kept aim. Sara made to run, but felt paralyzed. "You're going to pop this woman, the woman I love?"

Sara's gaze raced between the two. She assumed now Paul was mortal, as she prayed to her savior, unsure whether he was already in the room.

"You can't love her and, yes, I will defile her. Her virtue will belong to the Bourgeois clan. She killed the man they worshipped. It's their right, and then she will die."

"You better think twice about that." Paul pulled the trigger.

Jack Leroux fell dead on the bed. Sara still lay paralyzed in bed, naked, legs spread. Paul, in a burst of weakness, lust, or a combination of the infatuation bursting from within, took advantage of her. He dropped his seed, fertilizing any ovum which may have dropped.

"What did you just do?" Her eyes glowed, peering through his soulless body.

"We had sex. What the fuck do you think we did? That man is calling, and you best roll along. I'll see ya in Louisiana. We can marry now."

"We ain't getting married. Y'all ain't even a man." Other choice words followed, trying to regain her strength. She stomped through the saloon doors and ran into a Marshall. He was a brute of a tall, strong black man.

The Marshall followed them from Terrell, even though he wasn't allowed there after dark. He held a picture of a young girl.

"Finally found you. You're a wanted girl."

"For what?" she asked, her hands and arms covering her breasts and what they violated.

"Where shall we start the killings of a deputy in Sabine Parish, four ferry boat operators, a bounty hunter and the rancher Clarence Bourgeois? You know what? They were all related. I got to arrest you for the train robbery. I've been after the Leroux gang for quite some time." He stared hard, all business.

"The killings were all in self-defense." Her naked body shook as she tried to stay covered up.

"I want Jack and the kid, but I need to talk to you."

"Jack is dead. The kid was up in one room in the saloon. He raped me. It's why I'm naked."

"Don't leave," Marshall Reeves advised, before pacing into the saloon in search of the two outlaws.

Sara saw the Marshall ascend the stairwell. She sprinted towards the boarding house, wrapped herself in the blanket, and remained hidden on the wooden floor of the flophouse next to Kaydence's bed.

Rose's uncle burst into the room as the sun peered over the eastern sky. "Rise and shine, ladies. Rose, ready to see your home?"

"Are we gonna eat some breakfast first? Plus, I want to stay with Sara a little longer."

"I want to stay with you, too. You grew up on our adventure. I was impressed with you and what you learned." Sara said.

She was still naked, wrapped in the blanket while standing.

"You can stay here on the ranch," her uncle advised.

"No, we can't." Sara cut in. "Marshall Reeves is looking for us. Kaydence and I need to skedaddle. We can eat on the run." She whispered, so the others didn't hear.

"That was fucking Leroux's plan all along," he whispered back. "Get out of here, so I need to get Rose out of here. He's one bad mother-" He bit his lip since he was sober and there were ladies around.

Chapter 26

Sara and Kaydence rode on, following the Arkansas river towards the Choctaw nation. A place they would be welcome if they chose to reside somewhere besides the Caddo country. The land outside the future boom town flooded heavily because of recent rains, causing the horses trotting their way towards home to splash through puddles.

The return ride was uneventful. They slept in the hills and prairies, hunted and gathered their grub, trading pelts along the way. In no hurry to get back, they took their time, often spending an extra day or two to enjoy their time in certain areas. In East Texas, near the spot Sara made her jail break, they searched for a ferry. They sat in the bayou looking for fallen logs to build a canoe or a raft, where the horses could stand.

They searched the forest, hoping for enough fallen logs to carve something. Sara wandered deeper into the thicket for anything fallen the horses could aid in dragging the fallen timber.

The rhythm of the trees came to her. A tambourine played as the wind rustled through, calling her name. "Sara, Sara."

A familiar face appeared and screamed, "You killed him; you killed my lover. Your family will pay. Never you enter Texas again." She made her appearance, and the winds increased.

Sara stood still, unable to run against the easterly breezes that shared the same force as a tropical storm. Mattie had no problem circumventing the gale. She approached the still motionless Sara at the same time her hand reached for her revolver.

Less than twenty feet away, Mattie was no longer the beautiful cousin Sara first saw in Colfax, but a hellhound. It would take more than one shot, maybe several shots, to slow her down.

"I'm crossing the river. My family will only return with permission from your protector." She unloaded all six bullets into the beast. It didn't faze her and continued to close in. Sara grabbed the blade she had planned on using to skin a raccoon pelt they trapped earlier.

The hound leaped into Sara's blade and dropped beside her. The winds ceased as Sara sprinted back to her friend and their horses.

"No time for a raft. These horses can swim, Kaydence. Let's cross this river." As they hurried, she explained to her friend what had happened. On arrival at the river, she heard the pluck of a guitar in her head. The notes reminded her of the kid who raped her, the devil himself. She paused her horse, paces behind Kaydence, riding ahead. Words came to her in Paul's voice.

"That girl, she took it on her own,
I had nothing to do with getting that girl home.
Papa wants her to be in his family tree
"Her kin will forever believe in what I can be."

Another guitar broke, the tune soon fading. Sara shook her head, gouged the horse in the side to catch up with her friend.

Sara Barnum remained single, producing the one offspring, Cecil. Sara worked hard perfecting the whiskey, and when Cecil was four, he took to aiding his mother with cooking the brew.

Often the two were run off their land, either in Caddo or Creole country, but a permanent home was something Sara was never accustomed to. The duo bounced around Western and Central Louisiana, like a springtime tornado whips up the land, until Cecil found permanent dwelling north of Shreveport.

Sara Barnum went missing, presumed dead. A representative of a family living on the West side of the Sabine had followed her to the shack she shared with her only son. It took one slash with the machete for her head to bounce along the shore of the black bayou, before disappearing into the murk.

Rose grew up west of Tulsa on her uncle's ranch, and when she became of age, she fell in love with a man called Bittercreek. Bittercreek ran with the infamous Dalton gang, and Rose did her part in supporting the outlaw gang. Kaydence learned of both their stories, wrote them down, and published it in the Natchitoches Times. She worked at the Caddo Tribal Living History Museum until her death in 1936.